## Also by Mark Greathouse

**The Wolf's Tales**

The Wolf's Quest: Isa's Adventure Begins

The Frontier Calls: Two Spirits, One Adventure

**The Frontier Chronicles**

Perilous Trails: Jack's Adventure Begins

Wyoming Calls: Jack's Risky Quest

Longhorns North: Jack's Great Trail Drive

Warpath: Jack's Faith is Tested

Hunter Vs. Hunted: Jack's Great Frontier Challenge

Freedom Drovers: Jack's Awesome Crusade

A Poison Spreads: Jack Seeks the Antidote

Darkness Looms: Jack Faces War

**The Tumbleweed Sagas**

Nueces Justice

Nueces Reprise

Nueces Deceit

Nueces Blood

Nueces Grit

Nueces Truth

Nueces Legend

**The Tumbleweed Sagas - Junior's Story**

Lone Star Vigilante

Guns on the Guadalupe

Railroad to Perdition

Nicholas Dunn: The Making of a Texas Legend (A Western Adventure)

# Wild Horses on the Laramie: A Life of No Boundaries

# Wild Horses on the Laramie: A Life of No Boundaries

The Wolf's Tales

Book Three

Mark Greathouse

**Wild Horses on the Laramie: A Life of No Boundaries**

Paperback Edition



WISE WOLF BOOKS
An Imprint of Wolfpack Publishing
1707 E. Diana Street
Tampa, FL 33610

wisewolfbooks.com



Paperback ISBN 978-1-968733-35-3 eBook ISBN 978-1-968733-34-6
LCCN 2026936055

*Dedicated with love to my wife Carolyn, our two sons Mike and Matt.*

*Love is patient, love is kind. It does not envy, it does not boast, it is not proud. It does not dishonor others, it is not self-seeking, it is not easily angered, it keeps no record of wrongs. Love does not delight in evil but rejoices with the truth. It always protects, always trusts, always hopes, always perseveres..*

—1 Corinthians 13:4-7

*Honor the Messiah as Lord in your hearts. Always be ready to give a defense to anyone who asks you for a reason for the hope that is in you.*

—1 Peter 3:15

# THE CAST

**Isa (a.k.a. Wolf) O'Toole**—*Sixteen-year-old son of Jack O'Toole, whose quest is to venture alone into the great frontier of the North Platte River country. Isa translates to wolf in the Comanche tongue.*

**Awentia (a.k.a. Morning Star)**—*Fifteen-year-old daughter of Lakota warrior Wapitiyu Okle (Spotted Elk) and granddaughter to Chief Lone Horn. She's married to Isa. They have a son named Moses.*

**Jack O'Toole**—*Father to Isa. Earned the Comanche name Pohya Isa, Walks With Wolves.*

**Blue Flower**—*Young sister to Spirit Talker and daughter to Buffalo Hump, she's married to Jack. They have three children: Isa, Peter, and Nadua.*

**George Freeman**—*A Black cowboy who establishes the Circled Cross Ranch on the North Platte River in Wyoming. Father to Esmeralda. Adopts Lakota child, Zebediah.*

**Running Waters**—*George Freeman's Pawnee wife.*

**Esmeralda Freeman**—*George's and Running Waters' ten-year-old daughter.*

**Zebediah Freeman**—*Foundling Lakota son of George and Running Waters.*

**Juan Perez**—*Creative, hard-nosed Mexican cook on Jack's trail drive.*

**Taabe**—*Wolf offspring of Zebediah. Alpha mate to Mua.*

**Wapitiyu Okle (a.k.a Spotted Elk)**—*Miniconjou Lakota who is Morning Star's father.*

**Will "Wally" Wallace**—*Elderly mountain man who roamed the wilds of the frontier.*

**Hap Cole and Dred Evans**—*Cowboys on George Freeman's ranch.*

**Lieutenant Wallace Dickerson**—*An officer in General Crook's 2nd US Cavalry.*

**Chester Donovan**—*First hand hired on the Laramie Cross Breed Ranch.*

**Connor Culthwaite**—*Ranching neighbor to Isa and Awentia.*

**Syd Booker**—*Man contracted to build Charles Guernsey's house.*

**Will Cutter and Joe Moon**—*Wranglers hired to work the Laramie Cross Breed Ranch.*

**Farley DeGrange and Kyle Jones**—*Former JA Ranch cowboys who aim to seek their fortunes in Deadwood, South Dakota.*

# Historical Characters

**Tatanka Iyotake (a.k.a., Sitting Bull)**—*Hunkpapa Lakota holy man and chief who inspired the plains tribes to fight the White settlers. His warriors help defeat General Custer at Little Bighorn.*

**Dull Knife**—*Northern Cheyenne chief and ally of Lakota chief Red Cloud.*

**Little Wolf**—*Northern Cheyenne chief and signatory to the Fort Laramie Treaty of 1868.*

**General George Crook**—*Based out of Fort Laramie in 1876, his assignment was to eradicate the "Indian Problem."*

**Charles Arthur Guernsey**—*A legislator, rancher, and mining promoter from Cooperstown, New York, who arrived at The Emigrant's Washtub in 1880 and for whom the town of Guernsey was eventually named.*

**August Klappenbach**—*Co-founder and early enterprising resident of Bandera, Texas.*

# Isa's journey from Texas to the North Platte River country

*The route used by Isa on his journey north from Texas as spawned from his vision quest. It featured challenging landscapes and many tribes known to be hostile.*

# Wild Horses on the Laramie: A Life of No Boundaries

# You are invited

Dear Reader,

A teen half-breed, a one-man pony, a warrior woman, and a wolf tame the 1870s American frontier. That about sums my story. If you're reading the Wolf Tales series, then it's likely that *Perilous Trails* and my pa's Frontier Chronicles series must have fully grabbed you. This third part of my tale begins in 1879, a few years after I left home on a vision quest. I am seventeen years old but a grown man by frontier standards.

*Wild Horses on the Laramie: A Life of No Boundaries* continues the testing of my courage, faith, endurance, pure grit, and search for a life mission that I share with my warrior woman wife, Morning Star. My folks named me Isa, which translates in Comanche to Wolf. I expect that I should add that my pa is White and my ma is a Comanche. That makes me, my brother Peter, and my young sister Nadua what folks called half-breeds. As you'll find out, this can be a blessing and a heavy burden. Do keep in mind that my story incorporates history not found in most school history books. This book relates my tale as driven by fate and guided by God.

I have met up with plenty of Indians, especially Comanche and Lakota Sioux, so you'll find me using some of their language throughout *Wild Horses on the Laramie: A Life of No Boundaries.* I have provided a handy glossary of Comanche and Lakota words toward the back of this book. I also provide a convenient glossary of frontier terms.

I'm a Christian, but I have tried to grasp the Comanche and Lakota cultures to better understand them. The Indian religion is based upon what is referred to as animism in which every common natural item from fish and animals to plants, trees, waterways, and mountains were believed to have souls or spirits. The spirits and traditions connected with them guided the Comanche and Lakota. Their passion for their spirits no doubt gave them their fearlessness as fed by the belief that they were protected in everything they did. Would they kill to defend their beliefs? Theirs was not a religion of love and forgiveness.

Could Indians like the Comanche or Lakota become Christians? My stories in the Wolf's Tales share my personal evolution at the intersection of faith and culture. It was like Saint Patrick's conversion of the Irish to Christianity, folding many of their less offensive heathen rites into the Catholic faith. Would this work with the Indians? Well, it's part of the story.

As you follow my adventures, ask yourself whether you might be up to meeting the challenges I take on. Dangers? Privations? Hmmm. How might you have fared? Through it all, I first relied on the teachings from my family, then went on to learn from the raw and risky experiences I faced. I learned to trust in instincts forged from my biblical lessons.

To be straight here, I had no idea that my story was going to fill multiple volumes until I began to write it all down. I invite you to follow my adventures on America's western frontier.

Kindest Regards,
Isa "Wolf" O'Toole

# Prologue

By this time, the remaining warriors from the frontal assault were nearly upon us. I saw Hap fall from a glancing warclub strike to his head. George was bleeding from an arm wound but holding his own, wrestling with a hostile nearly as big as he. Where was Chester? And Dred?

The Arapaho losses were heavy, but they were intent on delivering their insane savagery and obsessed with stealing those prized Quarter Horses.

Taabe and his pack went to work on the warriors attacking our frontal defenses. The Arapaho were learning that their fears of the mighty wolf were justified. The very sound of the snarling wolves and the snapping of bones ought to have weakened any sane human's resolve, but the Arapaho were committed to this battle. The frontal assault pressed on, and our makeshift fortress became a place of sweaty, bloody, writhing bodies in a clash to the death. We were small in numbers but seemed to be holding our own.

I saw Morning Star so close, I could reach out and

touch her, were I not battling Arapaho. Out of the corner of my eye, I saw her break open the side of a warrior's skull with the butt of her rifle. She was a raging mass of womanhood and proving every bit the measure of the attackers. Her knee came up and doubled over a hostile. She delivered a finishing blow to the back of his head.

The mortally wounded Arapaho still stood in my face. My deep slice across his chest oozed blood onto both of us. He smelled of the pungent aroma of battle. The savage's fingers strove to dig at my eyes, and his heaving chest pressed close to mine, as I worked my blade up between us. With a great effort, I plunged my knife up to its hilt under his chin. I felt him go limp. No sooner had I let him slip from my grasp than I felt the hot breath of another Arapaho close behind me. I turned. All went black.

# Chapter 1

## Rescue!

I can't say that I remembered being hit. Morning Star was close at hand, fighting as determined and tough as any man. The last thing I saw was the savagely-contorted, war-painted face of an Arapaho warrior with his warclub moving in an arc toward my head. I don't even know whether I ducked. Apparently, I didn't or not enough.

A star-studded sky and full moon greeted me upon awakening. I looked up through eyelids nearly swollen shut. My head hurt like it had been hit with a hammer. I mean, it hurt bad! It pained me to move my head. I felt a presence, and despite the throbbing ache in my head, I turned it ever-so-slowly to see Morning Star lying beside me and nursing Moses.

"You awake?" she whispered with a soft smile and decidedly relieved tone.

I blinked to try bringing her into focus. My eyes barely cooperated. "Wh...wh...where are we?" I managed to ask groggily.

"We not move you," she apprised me. "Lose plenty blood."

I groped for what to ask next. "Wh…wh…what happened?" I finally got out in a hoarse whisper.

"Warclub," she responded, pointing to her head, then to me.

I lifted my hand to my head and felt a bandage. "Ouch!" I said reflexively. I wouldn't be touching that spot again for a while. I gazed at Morning Star. "You okay?" I asked.

She nodded.

"Everyone else? Hap? George?" I pressed.

"Chester shoot Arapaho from behind. Kill many. Dred come. Bring Lieutenant Dickerson and blue-coats. Horn sound chase Arapaho away. George okay. He go home. Take Hap. He be okay, too. Chester take horses back to ranch."

In my temporarily enfeebled mind, I worked out that we'd all managed to survive. That was a miracle. Chester had snuck out the side of our shelter just before the attack and stealthily worked his way behind the charging savages. He had been able to pick Arapaho warriors off one by one. Dred's success in bringing the cavalry ultimately won the day. Dickerson's bugle-announced arrival ended the attack. At least a dozen Arapaho had been killed. "Taabe?" I asked.

"He good. Hit Arapaho that strike you. Warclub not hit full. Taabe kill Arapaho."

It didn't surprise me that Taabe would defend me. He'd saved my life by causing the warrior's warclub to miss its target.

Morning Star stroked my chin. "Awentia happy Isa live."

Had there been doubt as to my survival? I managed a

smile, though it hurt my ever-throbbing head. I'd missed out on the ending to the battle, but we'd been blessed that none of us had been killed. Engagements with Indians didn't always turn out like that. Even in my groggy condition, I reckoned that I'd need to heap special thanks on Donovan, Dred, and Lieutenant Dickerson. While every blink of my eyes and turn of my head reminded me of my head wound, I owed God for having put Taabe in my life and thus having saved it. I guess He wanted me around for a while longer.

I laid back and futilely tried to ignore the throbbing in my cracked noggin. My loved ones were close and safe. I succumbed to sleep.

* * *

I'd been moved. I had no idea when. It felt good to be lying in my very own bed. I tried to sit up. Nope. My head still hurt. I raised my hand to my forehead. The bandage was still there. Taabe lay at the foot of the bed.

Morning Star saw that I was stirring and came to my bedside.

"How long?" I asked.

"Seven days," she informed me. "Blue-coat doctor say you lucky to live," she added with a gentle smile. "I get soup." She turned to the kitchen. Apparently, the medical officer from Fort Laramie had visited at Lieutenant Dickerson's request, examined my head, and told Morning Star that my wound was extremely serious, and I was fortunate to have cheated death.

How right he was, as my head kept reminding me. "How about a steak?" I asked as she left the room.

Taabe looked up as though he understood what I was

talking about. I suspected he wouldn't mind a steak or two.

Morning Star turned with a smile. "Isa no chew."

I felt my jaw and realized that the blow to my head had jammed my mouth. It nearly broke teeth. My jaw wasn't quite ready to chow down on solid foods. "Soup good," I admitted. While she fetched the soup, I made a super effort and managed to sit up. Taabe arose reluctantly and nuzzled my leg as if to say he was glad to see me feeling better.

A combination of surprise and relief swept Morning Star's face as she approached with the soup. "Isa strong," she observed with a loving smile.

I would have laughed were it not for the lingering pain. "I had a dream," I shared.

Morning Star smile. "Isa talk in sleep. Dream of horse."

"So, you know," I said as enthusiastically as my condition permitted. "It's a handsome bay mustang stallion. We saw him on our way home from Cheyenne."

"Isa capture?" she asked.

"He won't be captured. He holds much spirit. I must win his heart." The trust of the bay mustang would have to be earned.

"Isa have strong spirit," Morning Star assured me.

"You have strong spirit, too," I said. I took a spoonful of soup and managed a smile. "Strong spirits must join together for great strength." I reckoned that the bay stallion would make my Quarter Horse-mustang breeds exceptional. As soon as I regained enough strength to ride, I'd be heading southward to find that stallion. I finished the soup with Morning Star and Moses looking on.

Morning Star went back to the kitchen. I heard a pot

clang on the stove and then the sound of meat sizzling. A few minutes later, she brought me thinly-sliced pieces of steak, mashed to tenderness. "Isa try this," she said softly.

The gesture brought tears to my eyes. I put a piece in my mouth and chewed slowly.

"Is good?" she asked.

"Is good. Awentia wonderful," I said from the depths of my ever-loving heart. I polished off the rest of the steak and belched.

Morning Star laughed as she took the plate. "Isa get rest. Soon ride horse."

I wasn't going to resist her advice. Oh, but that meat had been God-sent.

* * *

I so dearly yearned to bring that bay stallion to Laramie Cross Breed Ranch. His spirited gallops across the prairie haunted my dreams. In my mind, he belonged here with our Quarter Horses. Alas, the bay surely had other ideas.

My head finally stopped aching enough to ride. Over the past few days, I'd made several visits out to the barn to visit with Paint. His nuzzlings and responses to my caresses told me that he was ready for me to saddle him up and head off on new adventures.

"Today's the day," I announced to Morning Star at breakfast.

"Cold," she observed.

While my head had been healing, I'd nearly ignored the steady onslaught of winter. Only my trips to visit with Paint served to remind me of ever-chillier temperatures. It was already late September, and we hadn't seen the first snowflake. I didn't reckon that bode well. It was like a calm before a storm. We might not see the snow depths far to our north, but wind-driven blizzards and drifts could be life-threatening. "I'll dress warmly." That meant I'd don my bearskin coat.

"No Arapaho today," deadpanned Morning Star.

I laughed at her humor. It was the first time laughing didn't make my head throb.

"Isa be careful." She was concerned that I not rattle my brains around any more than necessary aboard Paint. The Arapaho warclub had likely done more damage than any of us cared to admit.

I quaffed the last of my coffee, kissed Morning Star and Moses, and grabbed my bearskin coat, hat, gloves, and trusty Winchester.

I opened the door, and Taabe was off like a shot. It seemed he'd been patiently awaiting my recovery. Now, he was already in a full run with his pack. I figured he'd be welcoming additions to his pack come spring.

"Going for a ride this morning, boss?" asked Donovan.

"Reckon so, Chester," I replied with a chuckle. I still wasn't used to being called the boss, especially by someone nearly twice my age. However, facts were facts. I realized that it was less about my strength and size, and more about whether I could manage and lead. My pa had taught me that anyone could learn to manage, but leadership was a very different quality. A leader inspired, led by example, and possessed a God-inspired servant thinking. Like the wolf, a leader was loyal, showed courage, was a ferocious fighter in defense of right over wrong, and possessed innate and learned wisdom. In my short lifespan, I'd mostly unknowingly striven to embody those qualities. I suppose the proverbial fruit doesn't fall far from the tree. I'm my pa's son, and he's a God-blessed leader if ever there was one.

I slipped a bridle on Paint, then hefted the horse blanket and saddle over his back. He pranced and whinnied just a tad with excitement.

"Where you headed today?" asked Donovan.

"South," I replied dryly, as though it was no big deal.

Donovan chuckled. He knew what I was up to.

"You want to join me?" I invited.

"Thought you'd never ask, boss," he replied.

We let Morning Star know that we were both headed out. Cold weather generally meant fewer worries about Indian hostilities and virtually no wagon trains headed past the Laramie Range. The dangers of deep snows, ice-encrusted trails, fewer game animals, and icy rivers were simply too great.

"You think we can capture the bay?" Donovan asked.

I chuckled. "Not today."

"How you figuring to do it?" he pressed. He wrapped his collar a bit tighter around his neck.

I let out a sigh that filled the air before me with frozen mist. "Trust, Chester," I said. "It's all about mutual trust. We've got to truly believe that we're not out to hurt each other. Fear must be overcome. I recall in Psalm 56, King David said, 'When I am afraid, I put my trust in you.' Trust is critical to overcoming fear. The bay is afraid of us."

"Makes sense. I never thought on how trust works in our lives," observed Donovan.

"I see trust as part of having faith in God," I shared.

"You believe that right strongly, don't you?" asked Donovan.

He'd never discussed faith with Morning Star or me, and I had no idea what he'd grown up with. "My folks have strong faith in God. I was brought up around it, and it's served me well."

"You think that Arapaho warclub not killing you was God's protection?"

I smiled, though it nearly cracked my freezing lips. I smeared some bear grease on them. "Arapaho, Kiowa, Cheyenne, Mexican bandits, bears, and more. God seems to be looking out for me, Chester." I slowed Paint through an icy patch of trail. "Do you believe in God?" I asked boldly. It occurred to me that I should have known his answer back when I first hired him, not that it would have been the only reason to bring him on board.

"Pretty much," responded Donovan.

I replied with as much of a questioning look as could be mustered in the cold.

"Nobody taught me anything. My folks never went to church. I left home young. I think I found God the first time someone shot at me. I have a hard time trusting anything or anyone." He paused in deep thought. "You and your wife have been the first folks I've felt I could truly trust."

Donovan had just delivered a mouthful. "Thanks kindly, Chester. We wouldn't want it any other way." I was about to say more, when he pointed to a half dozen horses about a half mile off.

"There he is, boss!" announced Donovan.

"Now, what I'm about to do might bore you to death, Chester. You don't have to hang around. If you do, you're going to have to be very quiet and very still."

Donovan gave me a curious look. "Okay. What do you have in mind, boss?"

"We're going to dismount and stand on yonder rise for about an hour. The bay is going to see us. He won't come near, but he'll know we're here." I slipped from my saddle. With my bearskin coat, the stallion might mistake me for an actual grizzly, but I wasn't figuring to freeze. The bay would adapt.

So, Donovan and I stood for about an hour watching the bay stallion. He saw us, as he ran his mares past a couple of times. He kept his distance at about a half mile off. He reminded me of the speedy and elusive pronghorns that would dance about tantalizingly a distance away and then bolt at the first sign of you moving toward them. The bay was sort of like that. My breath condensed before my face. My toes and fingers were growing numb, but I endured.

Finally, I turned and nudged Donovan from his frozen torpor. We shook the blood flow back into our limbs and climbed into cold saddles. By the way, sitting a frozen saddle was no fun at all. We rode away with nary a look over our shoulders. I felt right good.

"How many times you going to do this?" asked Donovan.

"The bay has his territory. He'll get curious about the intrusion." I really wasn't so sure. I hoped I'd learned enough about wild horses that my strategy of gaining the bay's trust might work. The alternative was to gather a bunch of cowboys, rope off an area, and try to lure the mustangs into a trap. I didn't figure the bay would fall for that. He was smart.

The winter lay ahead, and I sensed it was going to be a rough one. I'd learned that the coats of these mustangs would grow thick in the winter and provide insulation. There was plenty of foliage around southeastern Wyoming that offered the increased food they needed to maintain body heat. It seemed that the digestive process actually generated body warmth. While I'd have loved to have given them the dry relative warmth of my horse barn, they would find the natural shelters to help them survive harsh conditions. When all else failed, they'd huddle together to share body warmth. Access to water was also important. There'd be enough accessible water from the North Platte and Laramie Rivers to supply the needs of the wild mustangs. They might have to break some ice, but they'd find what they needed.

"You're going to capture him, aren't you?" There was a tinge of disbelief in Donovan's tone.

I understood his doubt. After all, what did the Laramie Cross Breed Ranch have to offer a wild mustang stallion? Mares? He had them. Food? He had plenty. Shelter? He found what he needed. About the only thing special that I could offer was a safe home. The bay looked to be three or four years old. He must have figured out by now how to protect himself and his mares. This was going to take patience. "I reckon to bring him home, Chester. I don't think he'll be captured in the way you might think. He's got a spirit about him that defies capture. I'd sure like to breed that into our Quarter Horses."

Donovan appeared to be impressed. "I suppose that if anyone can do it, it'll be you, boss."

"I'll sure try," I responded. "Meanwhile, there's plenty to do at the ranch. I feel in my bones that it's going to be a tough winter. The livestock will need tending to. We've got plenty of food and firewood." We'd been busily stocking up before the Arapaho incident. I was glad that we'd built the house to enclose a spring. With a creek a hundred yards off, not having to break through ice and snow to retrieve water was a godsend.

"Mind if I head to Fort Laramie tomorrow?" asked Donovan.

I knew that he liked to keep up with his friends, still

wearing the blue coats of the cavalry. "Have at it, Chester. Enjoy yourself. Do check with Awentia to see whether she might need something from the commissary."

"How's your head feeling, boss?"

It was thoughtful of Donovan to ask. I realized it hadn't bothered me all morning. No throbbing. No headaches. "Thanks. You might tell the medical officer that I'm feeling right fine."

I guess I was officially healed. There was a scar to ever remind me of the scrape with the Arapaho warrior. There was a long Wyoming winter ahead, and being healthy would be important to our very survival. We were still a small ranching operation. We had our breeder Quarter Horses and mustangs, five head of cattle, a milk cow, a dozen chickens, and our trusty wolf-pack. We'd have to get them all through whatever the winter brought us.

Weather permitting, we'd occasionally travel to George's spread. As he'd just requested, Donovan would take time off to head to Fort Laramie to socialize with his former cavalry saddle mates over beers, cards, and shooting billiards. Life was only as boring as you allowed it to be. We spent a lot of time making and repairing clothes, tack, and tools. Weapons were kept in good working order, with guns always loaded. This was still the untamed frontier. Even in the midst of winter, trouble could happen. Shucks, it was only last winter that we saved Lieutenant Dickerson from freezing to death mere yards from our front door. Starving Indians or even a late-arriving wagon train could make life at the Laramie Cross Breed Ranch downright interesting.

Donovan and I soon found ourselves currying our horses in the relatively warm confines of stalls in the barn. My mind was still caught up with the bay stallion. I suppose it could be called an obsession. Obsession? Well, I didn't ride to the south pasture every day. While it could be said that I was indeed obsessed with the bay stallion, I did manage to tend to my ranch responsibilities.

Morning Star and I loved to cuddle up before a roaring fire after a day of chores and following one of her scrumptious dinners. We'd lie back on the buffalo rug and talk about the happenings of the day and our plans for the future. It didn't take me long to recognize that repeated rambling about the bay stallion failed to resonate well with my wife. Morning Star was pleased that I was dedicated to the horse, but a lot more pleased when I dedicated myself to her. I figured this out right quickly. Our time before the fire invariably became more than cuddling.

One sunny morning in early December, I coaxed her into wrapping Moses warmly in the cradleboard and joining me on one of my bay stallion vigils. She knew what she was getting into. She dutifully rode out with me and stood by my side, observing the mustangs.

The herd had altered its behavior slightly. The bay occasionally stopped and stared at me as though sizing me up. He'd look for a few minutes, sniff the air, bob his head a bit with an apparent whinny I was too far away to hear, and eventually gallop off.

Morning Star held Moses close to keep him warm. "He will come, Isa. I feel it, too." Her words were reassuring. Morning Star genuinely shared my passion for the stallion, she just wasn't so willing to stand in freezing temperatures to win him over.

I wasn't so caught up in my passion for the bay stallion that I was unaware that my loving and loyal wife was shivering. We'd stood for about half an hour. I took a final look at the bay and turned to Morning Star. "Let's go home."

She smiled, then nodded vigorously and led the way back to our horses. I held Moses' cradleboard while she climbed into the saddle of her mare.

I sniffed the air. "We're going to get a storm," I advised. Paint snorted and bobbed his head as though he'd heard me. Despite their thick coats, I suspected that the horses would be glad to be back in the barn.

"It is in the air," observed Morning Star with a nod of agreement.

# Chapter 2

# Blizzards

It was well before sunrise, and the fire was dying. The noise from wind-driven ice beating against the house awakened me. I extricated myself from Morning Star's loving arms, stood, shivered, and placed a couple of logs on the fire. I stoked it up a bit. Welcomed warmth was soon radiating throughout the house.

I heated the stove and began the coffee brewing process. I accidentally banged the coffee pot against the cast-iron stove.

Morning Star sat up with a wool blanket wrapped around her. "Isa noisy," she said through sleep cobwebs. She paused to listen to the raging blizzard, considered it, and snuggled back in her blanket.

We heard a plaintive cry from Moses snug in his cradleboard. "Me feed Moses," Morning Star said resignedly, wrapping her blanket tighter and padding off to settle our baby son.

"I'm going to check the livestock," I said, as I donned the bearskin coat, heavy moccasins, gloves, and hat. My Colt revolver hung in its holster beside the door. I was going to leave the rig, but grabbed it anyway and strapped it on.

Morning Star shuddered at the blast of cold air, as I opened the door and headed to the barn. Sensing a coming storm, we'd brought the livestock into our barns as protection against the anticipated blizzard. We'd run a colored rope from the house to the barn, like what George had done at his ranch. It kept us from going astray in a blinding snowstorm.

Donovan had gone to Fort Laramie, so I reckoned he was safe from the storm's ravages and enjoying reverie with his former cavalry saddle mates.

I picked up the rope and followed it hand over hand to the barn. The storm was downright wicked in its ferocity. I reached the barn and found Taabe and his pack huddled alongside the door. With their thick fur coats, they were pretty much immune to the storm. As I went to open the barn door, I saw that the pack was feasting on the haunch of an elk. It was reassuring to know that my wolf companions were well fed. Distracted by Taabe, I didn't see the windblown footprints in the icy layer in front of the door.

I walked around the barn making sure the livestock were in good shape. I went to muck a stall, but the horse leavings were frozen solid. It wasn't my favorite task and took considerably extra effort to get the job done.

I laughed at the chickens. They looked to be too cold to lay eggs. If the animals could think, they'd surely be appreciative of our sheltering them from the blizzard. They instinctively sought shelter, so perhaps they recognized their good fortune in being protected from the frozen blast.

For no particular reason, I decided to check the loft. Just before stepping onto the ladder, I happened to see icy dirt smudges on the lower rungs. I stepped back. Despite the cold, I shed my bearskin coat. I drew the Colt, took a deep, bone-chilling breath, and began cautiously climbing the ladder.

Reaching the top, I raised my head just high enough to scan the loft. My eyes widened at what I saw. "Chester?" I finished my climb and strode over to my ranch hand. "What are you doing up here?"

Donovan was passed out and shivering. His wet clothes weren't helping. "Wh…wh…what?" he managed through chattering teeth. He quite obviously was less than half conscious.

"Where's your horse?" I asked.

There was no response.

I smelled alcohol on his breath even from a couple of feet away. I couldn't believe that his trooper friends had allowed him to leave Fort Laramie. I sighed. "Let's get you down from here and into the house," I said while hoping he could withstand the hundred-foot walk through the storm's fury.

It was a struggle. With the help of a rope wrapped around us and looped over a rafter, I managed to get us both down from the loft. I fetched a couple of horse blankets and wrapped them around Donovan. They failed to stop his shivering. "Chester, this won't be easy, but we're going to the house. It's warm inside. Once you thaw out, you can tell us how you wound up in the barn." It concerned me that he'd not found his way to the bunkhouse or our house despite the blizzard. I supposed that the storm, combined with alcohol, messed with his judgment and especially his sense of direction.

I donned my bearskin coat, wrapped my arms around Donovan, and guided us back into the force of the storm.

I couldn't even see the house for the first few steps. I was never so grateful for the guide rope.

The stiff headwind made it seem like forever to get Donovan to the house. The door had become iced over during my time in the barn, so I lowered my shoulder and plowed forward to open it. Donovan and I fell inside, much to Morning Star's surprise. Fortunately, she'd gotten dressed while I was in the barn. Of course, Donovan was too far out of his wits to have appreciated it had she not been clothed.

Morning Star immediately came to our aid, helping me get Donovan seated in front of the fireplace where he could thaw out. Then, she dashed over to the coffeepot and poured a cupful for our near-frozen ranch hand.

Donovan was still shaking too much to hold the cup, so I put it to his lips. He looked at me gratefully, as the hot liquid began to thaw his insides.

"What happened?" asked Morning Star over her shoulder, as she returned to the kitchen to finish preparing breakfast. Of course, she'd add a third plateful.

Donovan looked at me through reddened eyes. He was beginning to recover from his cold-induced stupor. "I had too much beer. My mates worried about the blizzard and tried to keep me at the fort." He took a deep breath. "I figured I could beat the storm. Partway home, the storm hit. It was blinding right off." He paused again. He was now steady enough to hold the coffee cup, so he took another swig of the hot liquid. "I had to dismount to answer nature's call…pardon Mrs. O'Toole…and couldn't find my horse."

"And you made it to the barn," I added.

"I didn't even know it was the ranch barn. Somehow, I managed to climb up to the hay in the loft. I was wet and freezing cold. Guess I fell asleep. Likely would have frozen to death had you not found me."

Freeze to death? Donovan was right. He'd more likely passed out rather than fallen asleep. It was a fair assumption that he wouldn't have lasted but a few more minutes when I'd found him. Once a freezing body is unable to heat itself, death can occur with surprising swiftness. Call it God's will, but my heading to the barn early saved Donovan's life.

"I'm so sorry, boss. I was foolish."

"Lesson learned, Chester. The weather must be respected." The effect of the alcohol had surely clouded his judgment, as he was experienced enough to have known better than to race a storm. "Maybe, next time you won't be drinking so much," I chided. "Now, let's get you over to yonder table and get some grub into us all." My blessing over the delicious breakfast Morning Star had prepared was a bit more inclusive than usual.

* * *

In addition to ranch chores, I managed to keep up my visits to the bay mustang stallion. It was imperceptible, but I was making progress. If nothing else, I had captured his curiosity. He'd obviously endured the latest blizzard. I wished he realized that he could be enjoying a dry horse barn and access to my beautiful mares instead of an icy landscape. On the other hand, he was totally free. That was priceless by any measure. Still, I yearned to earn his trust. I even figured that I could bring him in for breeding and let him roam free after he'd mated with my mares.

*Old Man Winter*—I picked that name up from one of the troopers at Fort Laramie—wasn't finished. We'd endured a couple of snowfalls that didn't rise to blizzard proportions, when I awoke a mere two days before Christmas and stepped outside to that familiar feel in the air. We were planning to travel to George's for a Christmas celebration, but it was beginning to appear as though there'd be a hitch in that plan.

I reckoned that I had a few hours before the storm struck, so bade Morning Star farewell, saddled up Paint, and headed out to the south pasture.

I ground-hitched Paint and took my regular position at the crest of a low hill. I had been standing for about fifteen minutes or so, when the bay stallion appeared. He was running with four mares, when he came to an abrupt halt. He turned toward me and began to walk cautiously in my direction. Had curiosity finally had its way with him? I didn't move a muscle despite the bone-chilling cold that made me want to shake circulation into my hands and feet.

Step by step, the bay plodded toward me. Now and then, he'd pause and catch my scent. He'd give a snort and bob his head, then take a few more steps in my direction.

Amazingly, he came to within a couple of feet of me. He reached out his nose to catch a whiff of me. I read the caution driven by distrust in his eyes. The puffs of our breaths condensed in the frigid air and mingled. I dared to raise my hand to stroke his nose, but the motion startled him enough that he turned and ran off. I slumped with dismay. I'd come so close.

* * *

The blizzard hit the next morning. The weather didn't care a lick that it was Christmas Eve. I'd already checked the livestock, and we'd eaten breakfast, so Morning Star and I could now relax before the radiating warmth of our fireplace.

"Seems that we won't be visiting the Freemans today," I understated, as I gestured with my coffee cup. "Chester is celebrating with his friends at Fort Laramie. I don't think he'll try coming home in a blizzard again." I felt confident that he wouldn't do battle with Wyoming's icy blasts as he'd done a couple of months back.

"We have good Christmas here," Morning Star assured me with a wink and a smile. She snuggled closely. Moses slept soundly in his cradleboard. The groaning of the wind and the crackling from the fire were the only sounds. We were caught in the mesmerizing flickering of the flames before us. For me, it offered a moment of reflection.

It had been quite a year. Morning Star had given birth to our first child, Moses. Our first year of selling Quarter Horses we'd bred had gone reasonably well. The Comanche blood running in my veins led me to consider the dilemmas faced by the tribes in the region. Our own encounter with the Arapaho notwithstanding, the plains tribes were fighting losing battles with the US Army. Donovan told me that his trooper friends at Fort Laramie shared how Little Wolf and nearly four hundred Cheyenne men, women, and children had been defeated at the Battle of Punished Women's Fork in Kansas. They had tried to lure the soldiers into a trap, but a warrior gave away their position prematurely, and it led to the Cheyenne defeat. The survivors headed northward to friends and relatives in Montana, but most were captured or killed near Camp Robinson in Nebraska. Meanwhile, the famed Hunkpapa Lakota Chief Sitting Bull, remained ensconced near Wood Mountain in

Canada, where he'd escaped after Little Bighorn. There was no telling how much longer he'd stay there, as it strained relations between the United States and Canada. Worse for his people, the buffalo herds were smaller. The longer Sitting Bull lingered in Canada, the tougher the burden on his people. It struck me that the plight of the plains tribes was coming to an inglorious end.

"Isa thinking?" Morning Star broke my musings. "The bay?" she ventured.

I nodded and took a sip of hot coffee. "Not the bay," I replied with a slight grin and then grew serious. "Our people struggle. I feel the end may be near. They must follow White man's ways."

Morning Star nodded. "Is new world," she observed. "Even wild horses know."

That got me thinking about the bay stallion out in another blizzard. He'd endured worse, but I wished that he was in my horse barn. "I nearly touched him," I said. "He came this close." I raised my hands about a foot apart.

"He will learn to trust you," she assured me. "Isa strong spirit. God help."

I could surely hope that God would see fit to answer my prayers to ride the bay stallion. I was determined that I'd be riding on his back by summer.

"Fire warm. Awentia warm," she cooed and cuddled closer.

Praise God for my warrior woman wife.

# Chapter 3

## Bay Stallion

We were becoming ever more adept at breeding our stable of Quarter Horses and mustangs.

With meticulous record-keeping and careful pairings of stallions and mares, our herd was expanding. Donovan was carrying his share of the work, and I'd even begun to think about the dream Morning Star and I shared of also running a cattle ranch back in Texas. I got to thinking that Donovan might be just the man to run that operation. However, my obsession with the bay mustang stallion had to be dealt with first and foremost.

With winter ended, my venturings out on the range to try to connect with the bay were a tad more comfortable. Snow still capped the Laramie Range, but greenery was sprouting. Warmer weather was on its way. The Laramie River swelled with life.

"Today is the day. I feel it in my bones." I was pretty sure of myself.

Morning Star smiled enigmatically.

"What?" I asked.

"You feel horse in bones. Awentia feel child inside." She smiled at her revelation.

"You mean?"

She nodded vigorously. "No bleed. We have another O'Toole."

This was all the more reason to grow the Laramie Cross Breed Ranch and get the Texas operations started. There's nothing like a growing family to provide incentive. I harkened back to my pa's quoting Genesis 1:28, that we fruitful and multiply; fill the earth and subdue it. We were doing our level best to comply. My vision quest was being fulfilled bountifully.

"Isa happy?" implored Morning Star.

I realized that my thanks to God had caused my mind to drift away from the special moment at hand. "Happy? Isa is very happy." I hugged her and twirled her around the room. We fell together on the buffalo skin rug, and I showered her with kisses.

At a pause in my celebrating, Morning Star gazed deeply into my eyes. "Awentia love Isa very big." Her kiss consumed me.

I finally managed to ride out to my usual spot. There he was. It was as though he was waiting for me. As I dismounted with my back to the bay, Paint snorted and whinnied distractedly. Even a sugar cube didn't settle him. I turned and found out why. The bay stallion stood a mere dozen feet from us.

I reached into my pocket for another sugar cube and slowly extended my hand toward the big stallion. I knew that horses had a highly developed sense of smell. Paint's sense of smell had saved me from danger more than once.

The bay took a tentative step toward me and sniffed at my hand. He was still a couple of feet from me. I had a chance to truly study his face. His wild mustang spirit, the very core of his strength, was written all over it. His eyes were alive with the fires of life and his ears perked high.

I held my ground ever so patiently. Blessedly, Paint didn't move. He'd been around my breeder stallions enough that another male cayuse was no bother to him.

The big bay mustang nodded as though recognizing me as a non-threat. After what seemed like ages, he extended his head and licked the sugar cube from my hand. He gave me a surprised *what was that* sort of look. There was no question that it pleased him. But with another nod, an appraising once over look at me, and a playful whinny, he pranced off to join his mares.

I was in shock. All the hours I'd spent patiently courting him had begun to pay off. We'd made a connection. I was apparently finally accepted by the wild horses on the Laramie.

* * *

"He took the sugar from my hand!" I said excitedly upon entering our house.

Morning Star smiled. "I know. I felt it."

I gave her a doubtful look.

She smiled. "Awentia feel what in Isa's heart," she clarified. She read me the instant I walked into our home.

"It won't be long. He'll follow me here. I'm sure he

will." I knew in my very bones that I'd won over the big bay mustang.

"Isa name horse?" inquired Morning Star.

I hadn't given it a thought. In fact, he really wasn't mine to name...not yet. "I'll pray on that." When the time came, the name must befit the spirit of the bay stallion.

Morning Star handed me a cup of coffee. "No see Taabe today," she remarked casually.

I didn't see Taabe disappearing as especially concerning. "I saw the pack this morning. They were running down an elk calf."

Morning Star nodded. "Donovan say Shoshone and Paiute beat war drums west of Yellowstone."

We were partial to the Shoshone, as their descriptions of terrain and landmarks helped guide us through Yellowstone National Park. "I hope and pray they do not fight. Many will die, and they cannot win." I thoughtfully sipped my coffee. It was frustrating, as we were too far away to have any influence. As usual, it was a consequence of Whites settling the land, building towns and railroads, bringing diseases, and reducing the herds of deer, elk, and buffalo that were the Indians' food sources. Treaties were broken by both sides. It was little wonder that conflicts brewed across the land. I wondered what might have been the outcome if prejudices were overcome and promises were kept?

* * *

Morning Star placed dinner plates filled with the bounty of our efforts on the table. They were a sharp contrast to what many folks, especially many reservation Indians, experienced. "We hunt tomorrow?" she asked. "Need meat."

I nodded while glancing at her growing belly. Despite carrying our second child, she would keep up with me on mountain trails and handle carbine or bow and arrow as well as most any man; most of them better. "We hunt," I agreed and shoveled a forkful of scrambled eggs into my mouth.

* * *

We set off early, leaving the ranch chores to Donovan. The weather was warming, though snow still sat on the mountain peaks. We wore buckskins and moccasins, both for camouflage and quiet travel. We both carried bows and arrows along with our carbines. We took one of our pack mules, as we were confident that we'd have to carry out a lot of meat.

Heading up the North Platte River toward the mountains, we hadn't gone but a few miles, when I spotted a herd of whitetails. Now, we needed to draw close, as we had in mind using bow and arrow rather than gun and bullet. Importantly, we were downwind. We tethered the mule and began stalking the deer.

We spent the next hour creeping close enough to make effective use of our arrows. We eventually found ourselves squatting silently behind a sage bush within fifty feet of a beautiful whitetail buck. I nodded to Morning Star.

She'd already drawn an arrow slowly from her quiver and nocked it. She pulled back the bowstring, aimed, and let fly.

The startled buck looked up wide-eyed. He couldn't see the arrow buried deeply in his chest. He took a half dozen strides before his forelegs buckled and he keeled over on his side to breathe his last.

"One arrow!" I exclaimed. "Awentia shoot good."

She smiled and gave me a light kiss before heading to verify her kill. We were soon field dressing the buck and soon had the carcass draped over the back of the mule. We would be feasting on venison for several days, and Morning Star would make venison jerky. It had been the sort of hunt that we hoped to eventually teach our children.

* * *

We arrived home from our hunt by mid-afternoon. Donovan was impressed with our hunting prowess, though it wasn't unusual.

"There's something you need to see, boss," he intoned seriously.

"What's up?" I asked.

"Come around behind the house with me, but be very quiet."

"Have you seen something?" I pressed. "Do we have time to offload the mule?"

Donovan smiled. "I'll take care of the mule. You and Awentia go. You can't miss it," he said with a broad grin. "I didn't want to disturb it, knowing how special it is to you," Donovan was being purposely circumspect. He took the mule's tether and motioned us to head around the side of the house.

Morning Star and I exchanged curious glances and proceeded as Donovan had directed. We had no idea what to expect. We tread ever-so-silently. The senses we'd been using on the morning's hunt came into full play.

Our jaws dropped at the sight before us.

The bay mustang stallion stood near the corral, looking over the mustang mares inside.

"I'd best go alone," I advised Morning Star. I realized that I had no sugar cubes on me. They weren't something we generally brought along on hunts. I reckoned the bay was going to have to overlook the special treat. I began walking slowly toward him.

My, but he was handsome. The afternoon sun lent a majesty to his dark coat and rippling muscles. He fully exuded wild horse spirit in every fiber of his body.

He saw me. There was a tense pause. He finally nodded and pranced around in a circle before trotting toward me.

"Mukue," I whispered. *Mukue* translated to *spirit* in the Comanche language.

Mukue bobbed his head, then came close enough for me to stroke his forelock. He didn't pull back.

I gently patted his neck.

He almost tenderly nuzzled my hat off before pulling back, giving a whinny, and galloping off.

I stood transfixed.

Morning Star moved beside me. She picked up my hat and handed it to me.

I looked at the hat with near reverence.

"Bay trust Isa," she observed.

"Mukue. I have named him Mukue. He is the spirit of the horse." I was still staring off at Mukue joining his mares in the distant fertile plain.

"Mukue?" she queried.

"Comanche word for spirit," I shared.

"Is good strong name."

I realized that Mukue was interested in more than sugar. His was not idle curiosity. He was aiming to meet our mares. I expect his little herd simply wasn't enough for a big, strong stallion. "Pa taught me that trust overcomes fear," I said to Morning Star.

"Isa's pa a wise man," she responded.

I took one more look at Mukue. "Let's help Donovan with the venison."

* * *

We headed to the barn where Donovan had skinned the buck and was dividing the cuts of venison.

"That was quite a surprise, Chester. Thanks."

"How'd it go, boss?" he asked.

"He let me touch his nose and pet his neck. I think he's got a hankering for the mares." I chuckled, as I joined Morning Star in helping cut manageable pieces of venison. "Named him Mukue."

"Comanche word, isn't it?" responded Donovan.

"Yes. It means spirit."

Donovan nodded. "Well, Mukue has enough spirit for every cayuse at Laramie Cross Breed Ranch."

As I turned to cut a piece of the buck, I heard a whimper. I stood. "You hear that?" I asked.

There was another whimper.

"Sounds like a dog," observed Donovan.

"Or a wolf!" I exclaimed as I spotted Taabe limping into the barn. He was covered in blood.

"Where pack?" cried out Morning Star.

Taabe collapsed in the doorway. My God-given companion was badly hurt. Taabe had always been my great defender, but now he was the victim of a human's gun. Where indeed was his pack?

I rushed over to him and kneeled at his side. I examined his wounds. "My God! He's been shot!" I declared. I'd taken the Lord's name in vain, but felt sure I'd be forgiven. The wounds were serious but didn't appear life-threatening. He'd been struck at least three times. This was the real world, and there was no escaping from it.

"Let's get him inside the house," urged Morning Star. "We must treat his wounds."

Just as I'd become familiar with Comanche medicines from my ma and pa, Morning Star was well-schooled in the healing poultices of the Lakota. Taabe whimpered pitiably as I gently lifted him and carried him inside.

## Chapter 4

# Wolf Problem

Our elation over the bay mustang had shifted to heartfelt concern over the wolf that had been part of our lives since my vision quest.

Taabe lay semi-conscious on our kitchen table, as Morning Star gently cleaned and treated his wounds. He'd lost a lot of blood. She applied poultices and bandaged him as best she could. The lingering question was where was the rest of the blood from? It wasn't all from his gunshot wounds. Where were Mua and the pack? What had happened that he had gotten shot? I feared the worst for the pack.

We laid Taabe on blankets beside the fireplace. Despite his weakness, he struggled against sleep but eventually succumbed to it. Morning Star and I stood watching him. He seemed to be breathing steadily. I knew that Taabe was a wolf and not a dog. His instincts were decidedly different from tamed dogs. I daresay, he was smarter. I had to always remember that he was a wild predator near the top of the hunters on the frontier, along with the mountain lion and the bear.

We cleaned up, then I went outside. It occurred to me that there might be enough of a trail of blood that I might locate where Taabe had been attacked. There was still no sign of his pack.

I took a walk around the house, scanning the ground for any sign worthy of tracking. There were drying drops of blood that I assumed to be from Taabe.

Morning Star joined me. "We follow sign?" she ventured.

I nodded. "Let's get the horses."

Donovan emerged from the barn as we approached. "How's Taabe?" he asked.

"Weak. He lost a lot of blood, but he's sleeping now." I appreciated that Donovan understood the bond we had with the wolf. "We're going to try to follow his trail. Perhaps, we'll find out what happened. Please watch over the ranch while we're gone."

"What if Taabe awakens?" It was a logical question.

"He's familiar with you, Chester. Give him some water."

We saddled up and rode off, quickly picking up Taabe's trail. The sign took us westward. It was familiar ground. To our knowledge, there was only one homestead in that direction at present. It had been claimed by a family that had chosen not to continue on to Oregon. I'd seen the husband from a distance a time or two, but we'd not yet met. George knew of them from the wagon train that they'd separated from and told us that they had four children. He didn't recall their name. George told me that they were hoping to raise cattle but were inexperienced. I reckoned that their first challenge had been enduring their first winter on the Laramie River.

The blood sign was easy to follow. "Taabe bled a lot," I observed.

"Strong spirit," responded Morning Star.

We rode for about three miles. I was ever-more amazed that Taabe had covered so much ground despite his wounds.

We crested a hill and spotted a line of cottonwood trees ahead of us. The blood sign looked to be heading straight for the tree line. We looked up to see a buzzard hovering, so urged Paint and Morning Star's mare into a canter toward whatever the scavenger was interested in.

Our horses began to bob their heads and flare their nostrils. The scent of death was in the air, and they didn't cotton to it much. As we drew closer to the site, we could hear snarling and growling. The scene finally came into view.

I'd had a gnawing suspicion about what we'd discover. It was worse. Five wolves were being devoured by coyotes and buzzards. I drew the Spencer carbine and fired three rounds in rapid succession, scattering the scavengers for the moment. We dismounted and walked over to the wolves. It immediately struck me that they lay side by side. Even with the coyotes pulling at the carcasses, it was clear that whoever had killed them had laid their bodies on the hillside. Upon closer inspection and despite the ravaging of the bodies, my suspicion that they'd been shot was confirmed. The pack had likely been slaughtered by the same gun that wounded Taabe.

There wasn't much we could do. We found Mua, or what remained of her, among the bodies.

"Who do this?" lamented Morning Star.

We shook our heads with grief and anger born of frustration. We mounted up.

"Hey! What you Injuns doin' on my land?" came a harsh voice from just beyond the tree line. A rough-looking man carrying what looked to be an 1875

Winchester emerged from the cottonwoods. It was the sort of weapon that could devastate a pack of wolves. "Git on back to yer reservation. You don't be messin' with White man's land!" he exclaimed.

I took a long, measured look at him. "Put that gun away, mister," I ordered authoritatively. "Those cottonwoods mark the property line of the Laramie Cross Breed Ranch."

He obviously didn't expect to hear us reply in English. "Who you be to give me orders?" he demanded.

"I'm Isa O'Toole and this is my wife Awentia. We own the land you're standing on," I replied.

He gave us a curious look. "You a breed?"

I sighed. "We breed Quarter Horses. Now, lower the gun, whoever you are," I ordered again. Staring down the muzzle of that Winchester was decidedly unsettling. I sized the man up as not really wanting to shoot another human being. I sure didn't want to shoot him.

He reluctantly aimed the muzzle downward. "My name's Connor Culthwaite, and this here's my spread," he informed us with an angry look and a thumb pointing over his shoulder beyond the cottonwoods. His eyes caught sight of the rifles dangling from our saddles. He had to figure we weren't to be trifled with.

"Well, now that we're acquainted, did you have anything to do with killing these wolves? I inquired.

"I shot every danged one of them. Only one got away," he boasted. "And I nearly got him!"

Anger began to seethe within me at his bragging. Such was my near-human relationship with the wolves that in my mind, Culthwaite was no better than a murderer. Morning Star placed her hand gently on my arm in an attempt to calm me. I took a deep breath.

"Why?" It was a natural question that lingered in my mind.

"They attacked my son," he claimed.

I sighed. This conversation could get difficult. "How do you know?"

"Why the question?" Culthwaite asked.

I was trying to hold myself together. I silently prayed to God to help me stay calm. "It's an easy question, Mr. Culthwaite." I yearned to wrestle the Winchester from him and beat him with it.

"My son is near death's door. He's got deep claw cuts and bites that near caused him to bleed to death. Plenty of bruises. Had to be them wolves." He motioned toward the wolves with the carbine.

"How's your son now?" asked Morning Star.

Culthwaite was obviously surprised to hear Morning Star speak perfect English. "Er…he be hurting. Not too good."

I knew I had to forgive this man for his ignorance. It wasn't easy. It was all I could do to contain my passions. "Can we see him?" I pressed.

"Who you think you be to nose around?"

I sighed. We were eventually going to have to reveal our connection with the pack. "We know these wolves. They fear humans." I dared not tell him that the wolves would only attack folks who threatened Morning Star and me. "I don't think they attacked your boy. Wolves don't attack with claws. It sounds like a bear."

Culthwaite groused a bit and shuffled his feet. "The evidence be on his poor hurtin' body," he insisted but was caving to us bit by bit. "I be certain twas them wolves."

"Please?" I asked gently but insistently. "My wife has

medicine that might help your son." I hoped to reach some soft spot within him.

He gave us a studied once over. "Okay, come along," he groused. He turned and headed toward the family cabin.

* * *

Since Culthwaite didn't have a horse, we walked our cayuses. That gave us a chance to get acquainted with him over the next twenty minutes or so. We learned that he and his wife had fallen in love with the North Platte River country and decided to separate from the wagon train. They planned to raise cattle, but hadn't purchased any stock as yet. They'd farmed back in North Carolina, and he did some smithy work, but a flood forced them to give it all up and seek new opportunity. Their four children ranged in age from four to twelve; three boys and a girl.

We soon stood before their one-room log and sod cabin. Smoke curled skyward from a sad excuse for a chimney.

"Matilda?" he called. "We got company!"

We hitched our horses and patiently waited for Culthwaite's wife to let us in. Morning Star pulled a leather pouch from her saddlebag and checked inside it. We always carried the makings for poultices in our saddlebags.

The door opened, and a woman appeared who was likely younger than her haggard facial features and tired posture hinted at. The daughter and one of the boys bailed through the doorway on the run. "What is it, Connor? Johnny's ailing an' you done run off," she scolded him, then looked at us. "Holy Mother of God, we under attack!" she exclaimed, wide-eyed and half-ducked behind the rickety door.

"It's okay. They be neighbors," explained Culthwaite.

"Pleased to meet," offered Morning Star. "I am Awentia O'Toole. My husband is Isa." Her calm tone seemed to ease Matilda a tad. "We come to see your son. I bring medicine." She showed Matilda the pouch.

Matilda Culthwaite gave us a suspicious look. "Medicine?"

Culthwaite had had enough with the delay. His son was dying. He pushed past Matilda and led us into the cabin. The interior was dimly lit as was typical of these sorts of cabins. There were a couple of pieces of fine heirloom furniture they'd hauled with them from back east. Johnny lay on a bed at the far wall, although far wall was an exaggeration, as the cabin was no more than a dozen feet wide. That it housed six people was a testament to whatever drove these folks to want to carve a life out here on the frontier.

Morning Star and I eased over to the bed. Johnny was more unconscious than asleep. His wounds had been cleaned but were mostly exposed and untreated. The boy suffered a fever. Left as they were, his wounds would likely become infected and cause a slow death.

It was clear that the boy had been attacked by a bear. Wolf claws didn't compare to a bear, especially the grizzly that had left poor Johnny Culthwaite for dead. Grizzly claws could reach more than three inches. Unlike wolf claws, they were meant for grasping prey. The boy was lucky to have survived. "These wounds are definitely from a bear, Mr. Culthwaite," I advised.

"You mean?"

"The wolves were innocent."

"Well, they'd eventually kill something...maybe our livestock."

I shook my head. "The pack leader came to our house. He is my friend. We treated his wounds, and he will recover. But his heart will be broken."

"Really, Mr. O'Toole?" said Culthwaite incredulously. "Does it really matter?"

"He and his pack have been with us for three years."

Culthwaite's demeanor began to change. He appeared to be beginning to understand.

"Wolves hunt mostly old or very young animals or those weakened by illness. They fear humans. If very hungry, they may prey on cattle or sheep. If no wolves, there would be too many elk and deer and buffalo." I tried to explain how there was a balance that predators like the wolf helped to maintain.

"I...I'm sorry," lamented Culthwaite. "I didn't know."

By now, Culthwaite's wife had gathered her children and joined Morning Star. "Will he live?" she asked tearfully.

"Wounds very bad," confessed Morning Star. "Medicine help. You make soup."

I thought back to stories I'd heard from my pa about a famous mountain man fifty years ago named Hugh Glass, who survived a devastatingly brutal attack by a grizzly. Left for dead, it took him months to recover.

Matilda looked hopefully at Morning Star and then pleadingly to her husband.

"We be short of food," Culthwaite admitted. "Got no soup fixings." Those had to be among the most difficult words the man had ever been called upon to speak. No man cared to admit to failure.

Here was a chance to not only forgive someone who'd committed a dreadful wrong but help them as well. I turned to Culthwaite. "Hitch your wagon. We must bring Johnny up to our home. He'll have a better chance there." From the depths of my soul, I knew that I had to help these folks. It was as neighborly as it was Godly and downright practical. Johnny wouldn't survive under the conditions here in his own home.

Culthwaite and I left the cabin and walked over to the big Conestoga wagon they'd traveled in from St. Louis.

"This all you've got?" I queried.

He nodded. "And only one ox. We ate the other one," he admitted.

Fortunately, we didn't have far to go and wouldn't have to carry much of a load. We hitched the ox, then gently carried Johnny to the wagon bed and laid him on blankets.

The land between the Culthwaite's spread and our house was rough. Even moving as slowly as possible, every jostle pained the wounded youngster. I prayed he'd survive the ride.

* * *

Upon entering our house and laying Johnny on a bed comprised of blankets spread on a straw tick, we were greeted by a whimper from Taabe.

Culthwaite's eyes widened, as he realized that the wolf he'd wounded lay no more than six feet from him.

I could see regret looming large in the man's eyes, as he gazed at Taabe.

While Morning Star and Matilda saw to Johnny, I filled a bowl with water and walked over to check on Taabe.

Culthwaite's other two sons and his daughter

followed behind me with tentative steps. "Is he a real wolf?" whispered the little girl.

I nodded. "He is a timber wolf." I put the water to Taabe's mouth, and he drank. When he slaked his thirst, he licked my hand.

That brought a gasp of awe from Culthwaite's little girl. "He hurts like Johnny," she said. "May I touch him?"

"Touch his neck very gently." I took her hand and placed it against Taabe's furry scruff.

His smile was priceless. She turned to her father. "Did you hurt him, Papa?"

The pain in Culthwaite's eyes was full punishment. "I should not have," he told her. "I am very sorry. I thought the wolves had attacked Johnny. It was wrong of me. They were innocent."

The man had learned a life lesson. His thinking had been no better than vigilantes going after the wrong person as a consequence of overwrought passions. I wouldn't cotton to a wolf or any predator killing another human or my livestock, but killing out of misplaced anger and revenge was flat out wrong. I looked at Culthwaite's daughter. "What's your name?"

"I'm Tessie," she replied with a dimpled smile.

I looked up at Culthwaite. "Well, Tessie, don't be trying to pet these critters out there in the wild. You saw what the bear did to Johnny. Taabe here is a special wolf. But he is not tame like a dog. You must respect animals in the wild."

Tessie's brothers listened with total wonder. They were impressed that their sister had actually touched a wolf and lived!

"Connor, it looks like we're going to be neighbors for a while. We've lived here for a couple of years and have been blessed with plenty. By our faith in God and plain old human compassion, we believe that neighbors should help neighbors. It all balances out."

By now, I had Matilda's rapt attention.

Culthwaite shifted uncomfortably, as though he sensed what was coming. He felt totally undeserving.

"We have plenty of food stored away and aim to share some with y'all." I turned to Culthwaite. "You get your forge set up. I'll be needing horseshoes."

Tears streamed down Culthwaite's cheeks. "I...we... don't deserve...after the wolves."

"I said that I forgive you, Connor. I meant it. Now, let's be good neighbors." I shook his hand.

Morning Star sidled over to me. "Boy sick. He almost die."

"Will he live?" pleaded Matilda.

Morning Star nodded. "I think so. We all pray. Need God help."

"What gods do you worship?" asked Culthwaite. He still had our Indian heritage lurking in his mind. Prejudices weren't easy to fully wrestle out of folks' souls.

I pointed to the cross hanging above the long gun hanging above the fireplace mantel. "Only true God," I replied.

I began to say a prayer. "Lord, we lift..."

Just then, Donovan knocked and walked in. He'd seen the Conestoga and was anxious to check on our visitors. Importantly, he had other news.

* * *

"Sorry, boss," he called out to me. "Did you find the pack?"

"It's all taken care of, Chester," I replied. "This is

Connor Culthwaite and his family. They have that new spread west of us."

Donovan saw Johnny and was quick to pick up on what I wasn't saying.

"Anything else?" I asked.

"That bay has been nosing around the corral. He's out there now looking for you."

"Connor, Chester here will help you load up some supplies. I've got some business with a horse." With that, I headed for the corral.

# Chapter 5

## Riding the Bay

Johnny spent the next two weeks at our home. It was touch-and-go, as his body fought off infection and wounds healed. His mother came to visit nearly every day. If there were any lingering prejudices against Indians and half-breeds, not to mention wolves, the love and caring during Johnny's healing process surely dispelled them.

Culthwaite even came by and asked to go hunting. Naturally, I obliged. We tracked and brought home an elk.

Speaking of wolves, Taabe was up and around. He ventured outside but stayed close to home. If he was inclined to visit the spot where his pack had been massacred, he hadn't shown an inclination yet. He treated the Culthwaites as though they were part of our family. He made no connection between Connor Culthwaite and the demise of his pack. It ever amazed me at how Taabe could distinguish between friend and foe.

The bay stallion still occupied an inordinate portion of my thinking. That he regularly visited the corral had been a step toward building a more intimate relationship. I tried to remind myself that he was a horse, not a human. Yet I felt an ever-closer connection with him.

I guess it was the beginning of the third week of Johnny's recuperation. I was standing at corral stroking the bug bay and giving him an occasional sugar cube, when I felt Mukue tremble. He didn't move away, but his gaze shifted to something behind me.

I turned slowly. Johnny stood stock-still, staring at Mukue.

Mukue gave me a brief nuzzle and then walked over to Johnny. He sniffed the young man who eventually put his hand on Mukue's forehead. The bay stood motionless, as Johnny's hand stroked him.

For Johnny's part, a huge smile creased his face. It was the first show of anything resembling happiness since his attack by the bear.

I didn't know what to make of it. It seemed like a special moment. Perhaps, Mukue sensed Johnny's vulnerability.

After a few moments with Johnny, the big bay turned and walked back to me.

Johnny offered a wistful smile and limped back into the house.

I had the feeling that the boy's true healing was just beginning. It also made me aware that Mukue was a very special horse.

* * *

The time had come. Mukue's visits had become considerably longer. His mares even hung close by. I committed myself to climbing onto his back.

I hadn't a clue how I was going to go about this with

such a spirited horse. I felt as though we'd built a relationship of trust, and that there was strong communication between us. I used a currying routine that included wrapping my arms around Mukue's neck. I'd move toward his rump with my arms stretched over his back. I'd let him get a feel for my weight by increasing the downward pressure of my arms on his back.

Mukue was a big horse at what looked to be about seventeen hands at the withers, but I was no small fry as a human. At six-foot-three and well-muscled, I would be a load.

"Today is the day, Awentia," I declared at breakfast.

"Are you going to ride him, Mr. O'Toole?" he asked.

I nodded.

"He is ready," said Morning Star. "I feel it."

So it was to be. One way or another, Isa O'Toole was going to sit on Mukue's back...if he'd let me. "Y'all can watch from the house. I don't want to spook him."

"Spook?" asked Johnny.

"Frighten him. He trusts me."

With that, I took a final swig of coffee and headed out to the corral. Mukue stood beside it as though he expected me.

I walked straight to him and gave him a sugar treat.

He must have figured something was up, as he bobbed his head and gave an excited whinny. He nuzzled me and took a step forward so I could stroke his neck. He seemed taller than usual. Perhaps, it was because of what I intended to do.

"Are you ready, Mukue?" I gently asked.

He had gotten used to hearing his name.

I slid along his left side as I often did. This time I gently but firmly grabbed his mane at the withers and swung my right leg up over his back. He stood for a moment as though wondering what had happened. Where was I?

I expected he'd react as so many horses did. However, he stood still, as though trying to figure the sensation of a human on his back. He took a couple of tentative steps. When was he going to buck? I sat for another minute, then slid off. I stroked his forehead and gave him a sugar cube.

I glanced over at Morning Star and Johnny. They were smiling and making silent claps so as not to startle Mukue. Donovan joined them in the mock celebration.

I stroked Mukue a bit more, then turned to walk away. He bumped me in the back with his nose as though we weren't done. We were connecting at some level, and I think I had an idea on how to increase his interest.

"Chester, put that chestnut Quarter Horse mare in the breeding corral. Let's see if Mukue takes the bait." It was the first time I'd spoken in a normal tone of voice near him, but it didn't spook the big bay.

Donovan led the mare into the corral. It was a two-part affair designed to let the horses get acquainted. Once she was inside, I opened the gate to the other side. Mukue would have none of it, but he was taking a long look at the chestnut mare. His nostrils flared, as his nose absorbed her scent. Suddenly, he charged at the gate to her section of the corral. Timber went flying, and my handsome bay mustang stallion was on the mare and doing his thing.

When he'd finished, Mukue took off at a gallop for the south pasture with his mustang mares following. There was no *thank-you, Isa*.

I shook my head in dismay, as my audience enjoyed the show. "Go figure," I said. "No gratitude," I said, knowing he'd return.

"I write in log," said Morning Star.

"You keep records?" asked Johnny.

"We must record our breeding to ensure consistent outcomes," I explained to him. "It's part of the business. "If buyers expect high quality, then we are obliged to deliver it. We've already heard from one of our first customers that he wants more of our stock." I could see Johnny storing the information somewhere in his head. He seemed to be a smart kid. It appeared that he'd fully recover from the bear attack, but for some serious scars that would make for great stories to his children someday.

"I'm grateful for y'all taking care of me," said Johnny. "I expect that it's time to return to my folks' place. They sure need me."

"Your dad is a hard worker, Johnny. It's been a tough beginning, but he'll succeed. If y'all need anything, you know where to come."

Johnny looked at Morning Star and me with a sheepish expression. "Mind if I spend one more night? I'd like one more of Mrs. O'Toole's breakfasts."

"Why thank you, Johnny," responded Morning Star, her skin turning a deeper red with a blush.

Johnny looked at Morning Star and then at me. "I see you pray like White people," he observed.

"God give people different skin colors, but all bleed red, Johnny," counseled Morning Star.

"Why do they fight?" Johnny queried.

I smiled. "Good question, many answers. Red people live on land many years. They depend on land to live, grow food, and hunt. They move from place to place. But they hold territory by trade and ancestry. They fight each other, too."

Johnny gave me a confused sort of look.

"Whites come and wish to use land. They trap for fur, take gold, and build ranches, farms, towns, and railroads. Whites want to divide land and own it. Red man's land is everywhere. The Whites bring disease and kill much game. Some Whites think Red men are lesser people and treat them poorly. Red man fears loss of buffalo, deer, and elk. Treaties are made, but both sides break treaties. There is lying and cheating from White man and Red man. Homes are attacked. Soldiers fight great battles to protect White settlers." I was oversimplifying but felt that Johnny was grasping my teaching. "It's very complicated," I added.

"What about Blacks and Browns?" asked Johnny. He had seen our friend and former slave, George Freeman, visit and had seen some *vaqueros* from Mexico on trail drives.

"We should talk about this with your folks around, Johnny." I didn't even suggest discussing the Chinese labor used on the railroads. "The Freemans are coming to visit in a couple of days, maybe we can have a big feast and talk about this after we eat."

"I do want to learn more," he said.

"Now, I need to see to the mare that just got acquainted with Mukue."

"Thanks, Mr. O'Toole." He turned, then paused. "Do you figure to saddle-break that bay mustang?"

"I'm not sure. I want him to keep the free spirit he possesses."

He nodded and walked off.

Johnny had raised interesting questions about people, the *numunuu*, and about race. There was such an array of cultural and religious beliefs woven into how folks treated each other based simply on characteristics attributed to skin color. I headed to the corral to tend to the mare. As to saddle-breaking Mukue, I simply didn't feel the need.

* * *

The Freemans arrived late morning. I was anxious to show off Mukue to George. The bay mustang now came to the corral whenever I stood beside the corral gate. By now, I'd dissuaded the bay from expecting a mare or even sugar cubes with every visit.

With George standing beside me, Mukue hesitated to approach. Finally, I relented and held out a sugar cube. I stroked his forehead, then grabbed a handful of mane and swung myself onto his back.

"Oh my!" exclaimed George. "He's a beauty."

With a head bob and snort, Mukue permitted George to approach and pat his neck. "You going to saddle break him?"

"Nope. I don't want to ruin his spirit. I've been introducing him to the Quarter Horse mares." I smiled broadly. "We're going to make some cowboys very happy."

"You've come a long way, Isa. You and Awentia have a fine ranch. God's been good to y'all."

"And you, George." I proceeded to tell him about what happened to Taabe and the awkward introduction to our neighbors. "I've invited the Culthwaite family to join us for dinner. Johnny, the young man who recovered from the attack by the bear, has raised solid questions about life among people of different cultures out here on the frontier."

"Sounds like good after-dinner conversation," mused George.

"I reckoned that's what you'd have in mind," I said

with a broad smile. With that settled, my mind moved on. "You hear anything from Fort Laramie about the campaign to bring the tribes into the reservations?"

George nodded. "Sitting Bull is still in Canada waiting for things to cool off. The sense is that he'll eventually go to the reservation. He's done fighting. Other than that, the Bannocks and Paiutes under Buffalo Horn have been raiding settlements in Idaho and eastern Oregon. General Howard has been sent to get them under control. Lakota, Cheyenne, and Arapaho have been pretty quiet. That pretty much sums it up."

I nodded. George had covered a lot in summing up the challenges faced between the Indians clinging to their heritage and the waves of settlers bringing new life to the frontier.

* * *

Morning Star, with help from Running Waters, laid out a dinner spread that would long be remembered as one of the best ever. What likely made it most memorable were the children. Their energy was ceaseless. There was laughing and munching and slurping and belching and plenty of yummy sounds. It was good to see the Culthwaite family looking healthy and well-fed.

I watched the Freemans' daughter, Esmeralda, enthralled over Johnny Culthwaite's story about the bear attack and his wounds. Funny how girls could get caught up with those sorts of tales. Meanwhile, Zeb Freeman and Tessie Culthwaite were fascinated with our son Moses. Seeing the children interacting was heartwarming, especially given the mix of races that Johnny had been so curious about.

Once dinner ended, we gathered around the hearth.

George explained how it was an after-dinner tradition at his home to gather and discuss important issues and concerns or to pray. "I hear that Johnny here has some concerns about skin color." He said it in a tone that invited discussion.

Johnny glanced timidly from person to person. "Er...I was just wondering why folk that had different skin colors fight with each other?" He didn't hold back any.

"Why do you think that?" responded George.

That caught Johnny off guard. He squirmed a little. If he was seeking a flat-out answer, he was sorely mistaken. He thought a minute, while everyone turned to him with anticipation. "Well, Mr. Freeman...you...your skin is black, but I don't hate you. Mrs. O'Toole has reddish-colored skin, but I'm grateful with how she helped me heal."

George nodded. "That's the way it should be, Johnny. What would you say if I told you that many years ago I was a slave on a cotton plantation?"

"Slave?" asked Johnny.

"Yes. And my master whipped me. But I escaped and was taken in by Pawnees. They didn't care that I was Black. I met Running Waters, and we fell in love and were married. I worked as a cattle drive drover for a rancher. He didn't care about my skin color; only that I was a good cowboy. Now, I own a ranch and raise cattle. So, my skin color wasn't always a concern."

"Some folks are prejudiced," I added. "Some don't like me because I have Comanche in me, and they have something against Comanche. Others get angry, because some wrong was done to them by Indians. Many folks have a tendency to lump certain people together, like if Comanche attacked them, then all Indians are bad. Or, since most Blacks came to America as slaves seen as less-than-human, then all Blacks must be only worthy of a slave master's lash."

Connor Culthwaite offered a grim sort of smile. "Some think all wolves are bad, because they're ignorant about them," he said with a look over at Taabe.

The hearth session was good for everyone. We even talked about my connecting with Mukue. The trust the horse placed in me made for a comparison with trust in people.

# Chapter 6

## Wagons Rolling

With spring, the wagon trains resumed rolling through on the Oregon Trail. I say rolling guardedly, as the roughness of the trail took its toll on man, beast, and equipment. Many a wagon's load was lightened of heirloom furniture, as the Laramie Mountains loomed before the settlers. The trail was littered with broken wagon wheels and axles, bones of pets and livestock, and personal belongings found to be unnecessary. The saddest were the graves of those who'd never experience their western dreams. Some, like the Culthwaites, found that Wyoming met their vision.

It occurred to me that it had been awfully quiet so far as threats from the Indians. So long as Sitting Bull remained in Canada and the Cheyenne and Arapaho stayed on their reservations, it appeared that an unsettled peace would bless the land.

Situated as we were, north of the Laramie River but well south of the Oregon Trail, we didn't experience the wagon train traffic that passed the northern fringe of George Freeman's ranch. It hadn't been but a handful of years before that our ranch would have been set in the midst of Lakota, Southern Cheyenne, and Arapaho country.

Life seemed good. We'd settled into routines. Chester Donovan was a dependable ranch hand. Mustangs and Quarter Horses bred. Mukue visited frequently to enjoy treats and stay acquainted with the mares. He even permitted me to ride bareback. Moses had begun to walk, and Morning Star's belly began to grow with child. Yep, a good life indeed.

Good life until one morning. Standing before a front window and sipping coffee, I spotted a heavy column of smoke far to our north. I had a pretty good idea what it might be and dreaded what I might find were I to head north to investigate. "Awentia, come see," I entreated.

She peered out over my shoulder. "Oh! That very bad!" she exclaimed. "Who could have attacked a wagon train?"

It was a natural assumption. To our knowledge; however, there were no tribes nearby with sufficient strength to take on a wagon train. "I think Chester and I should ride up there and find out."

"Awentia go," insisted Morning Star. She was likely capable enough despite her pregnancy.

I sighed and nodded. "Chester can watch over the ranch," I said with a smile. She was ever my warrior wife.

We donned our buckskins, made sure our weapons were in working order, and were soon saddled up and riding northward. Taabe had recovered sufficiently to trot along behind us.

* * *

We rode better than four miles to the source of the smoke. The scene was bad but not what we expected. As we crested a gentle hill, we looked down upon about a dozen circled wagons. About half were in smoldering ruin. Folks, some apparently wounded, were milling around. There was no livestock. Horses, cattle, and oxen appeared to be gone.

We approached the circled wagons. As we got within about a hundred and fifty yards, two men strode out from the wagons and fired their rifles in our direction. Fortunately, we were beyond their abilities as marksmen.

I guess we looked threatening to someone who had just suffered an attack. Two riders in buckskins with a wolf accompanying them was likely a bit concerning. I pulled out a white cloth and waved it over my head.

The two men paused, lowered their guns, and waved at us to come forward.

As we urged our horses slowly forward, I continued to hold the white cloth high.

The men kept the muzzles down. "Who you be?" hollered one of the men. He gazed nervously from me to Morning Star to Taabe and back to me.

"The O'Tooles! Isa and Awentia!" I shouted. "We own a ranch back yonder," I said, motioning behind us. "We saw the smoke."

"Come on in," responded the same man tentatively. He seemed more worried about Taabe than us.

We finally arrived close enough to them to begin a conversation without raising our voices. "Who attacked you?" By now, we noted that several survivors had appeared between the wagons to observe us.

"They be Whites dressed as Injuns," lamented the

man. He held up what appeared to be a wig with a feathered headband. “My name is Clay Jordan,” he added.

Morning Star and I glanced at each other with surprise. “Your people hurt?” I asked.

“Killed two men and a woman. Couple others are wounded,” said Jordan. “They fired the wagons and stole all our livestock.”

“Which way did they go?” I asked.

“Hard to tell. I think they headed toward them mountains yonder,” said Jordan. He pointed toward the Laramie Mountain Range. “It was purty darn hectic.”

“I’m sure they be headed west,” interjected Jordan’s companion.

“Any idea how many attacked you?” I didn’t expect an accurate answer due to the confusion faced in the chaos of attack.

Jordan shrugged. “Too many.”

The fact that the attackers pretended to be Indians was concerning. I figured to inform the troops at Fort Laramie as soon as possible. “Can we come in? We have medicine for your wounded. We’re happy to help.”

Jordan motioned us to follow him to the circled wagons. “You Injuns?” he asked as an afterthought.

I nodded. “I’m half Comanche. My wife is Miniconjou Lakota. We raise Quarter Horses on our ranch.”

Jordan smiled. “My mother was half Shoshone.” He glanced at Taabe. “That wolf have to come?”

“Yes. He won’t bother anyone,” I assured him.

He led us within the circled wagons. Folks were milling around, still trying to take stock of their situation. “Wounded are over there,” he said, pointing to three women hovering over a couple of folks lying on blankets.

Morning Star dismounted, grabbed her medicine bag, and headed for the wounded.

The women tending the wounded were aghast at an Indian approaching.

"It's all right, ladies. She's here to help," Jordan called out.

I was still wrestling with White men disguised as Indians. I wondered where they intended to dispose of the livestock they'd stolen? I shook it off for the moment. "How many of y'all survived?" I asked. From what I could see, there were between thirty and forty folks gathered within the circle.

"There's thirty-eight of us," responded Jordan.

"You figure to continue westward?" I inquired.

Jordan nodded.

It was obvious that they'd be needing oxen and horses at the very least. "Y'all can backtrack to Fort Laramie to get oxen and horses. Might find a wagon or two, as well." I considered that a moment. "Y'all might join up with another wagon train."

"We'll have to do that, I expect," responded Jordan.

"We'd be happy to fetch our wagon you can use to take your wounded back to the fort. A couple look to be in bad shape."

"We'd be much obliged for your help," replied Jordan.

"I have a friend whose ranch you'll pass along the way. He may give you a good deal on livestock."

"We're much appreciative," assured Jordan.

"Y'all decide who is going to make the trek to Fort Laramie. My place is about four miles south over yonder hill. We can have a wagon here in a couple of hours that y'all can borrow."

"Borrow?" asked Jordan with amazement painted across his face.

"Yes. We trust that y'all will return it," I assured him. "Now, decide who is coming for the wagon."

Jordan gathered a handful of men. They buzzed with earnest conversation for a couple of minutes. Jordan broke free. "We're grateful to you, Mr. O'Toole. Our wagon master was killed, so they've elected me to be in charge. We're pleased to accompany you back to your place to borrow your wagon."

By this time, Morning Star had done all she could for the wounded. I filled her in on what we planned to do to help the settlers on the wagon train.

We headed back to our house, where we hitched a couple of mules to our wagon. We gave Jordan the reins and sent him back to the site of the attack so he could haul the wounded to Fort Laramie. Meanwhile, Chester joined Morning Star and me to discuss the man who'd posed as Indians to attack the wagon train and steal livestock.

* * *

"That Jordan fellow will warn the troops at the fort about the raiders," I reckoned. "However, what if they decide to attack local ranches in addition to wagon trains?"

"Good point, boss. But what are we to do? They likely have us outnumbered and outgunned." Donovan made good points.

"We cannot leave our homes, Isa," noted Morning Star.

They were both right. It wasn't as though we could pull a group of folks together at a moment's notice in such a sparsely populated region. What folks called a posse was not a workable option. I figured we could bring together Hap and Dred from George's ranch and Donovan from here at the Laramie Cross Breed Ranch. A posse of a half dozen of us seemed woefully inadequate. "By the time troops at Fort Laramie received orders to pursue the raiders, they'll have wreaked their damage and moved on," I postulated.

"It would help to know how many men the raiders have," observed Morning Star. It was obvious but needed saying.

Donovan and I nodded and shrugged. We were dealing with quite a dilemma. Then, an idea struck me. "The attack was only this morning. With all that livestock, especially the oxen, they couldn't have gotten far. I'm sure I could pick up their trail. I can surveil them and find out how many we're up against." There was no point in taking on the gang that attacked the wagon train unless we were sure of what we were up against.

Morning Star looked at me with a guarded posture. She dearly wanted to accompany me on any scouting expedition. However, with her pregnancy and baby Moses, she knew that her presence would put us in danger. "Isa go. Stay safe," she said by way of support.

"No time like the present. Chester, you hold down the homestead. I don't expect to be long." I reckoned to pick up the trail while it was still reasonably fresh.

Morning Star quickly pulled together some grub for the trail.

* * *

Wasn't long before I had Paint headed toward the wagons. Taabe trotted along with us. I was uncertain as to whether he'd accommodated the loss of Mua and the pack. Would he seek another mate? I waved to the folks among the wagons. By now, the wounded were already on their way to Fort Laramie, and the settlers were cleaning up from the attack as best they could. This included three burials. I expected that it wouldn't be long before they'd continue their journey westward. If I was lucky and God willed it, there was a chance that I'd recover their livestock.

I didn't engage with the settlers but went to work searching for the tracks of the gang that had attacked them. It didn't take all that long. Livestock have a way of leaving plenty of sign. There were too many hoofprints to get a feel for the size of the gang. Notably, all horses were shod.

The trail headed due west along the Oregon Trail for about a mile then cut in a northwest direction. This was country that I was very familiar with. They'd be limited by the livestock as to where they could camp. I sensed that they were aiming to shift southward at some point to reach places where that could dispose of their treasure.

I passed groves of aspen, stands of junipers, and clusters of cottonwoods. They'd been forced to take circuitous routes around steep hills and natural crevices carved into the earth's crust, while I could plunge on directly. I was able to leave their trail and pick it up again promptly. I also knew where any water holes lay, while my prey had to seek out larger bodies of water. I anticipated a place ahead where the North Platte River took a turn, and the gang would turn southward along the base of the Laramie Mountains. That's where I figured to intercept them. I stopped now and then to rest and water Paint. We'd then walk a mile or so before I rode again.

I was beginning to form an impression of the men I was tracking. I doubted that they fully appreciated the beauty, much less respected the land. It was unlikely that there was a God-fearing man among them. Their greed had driven them to attack a wagon train mostly peopled by vulnerable women, children, and men unaccustomed to the frontier. I doubted that the gang appreciated the wind singing through the trees, listened to the rush of the waters of the rivers and gurgles of creeks, or stood on a high hill to take in the majesty of God's creation. I couldn't help but judge them as simultaneously self-serving and self-loathing. Hatred, lust, envy, and sloth were their close kinfolk.

As the sun began to touch the western horizon, I caught sight of dust ahead and to my left. I'd surmised correctly. The bandit gang was headed south, where the markets for their stolen livestock were located.

* * *

My hunt now entered a new phase. I'd transitioned from tracker to stalker. My prey was spread before me. With daylight dimming, they'd be stopping right soon. A waning moon and plenty of stars meant that I'd have little trouble surveilling their camp. My challenge would be not being seen. That led me to wonder whether they were bright enough to post sentries. They were likely exceedingly confident that they'd not been followed by the settlers from the wagon train.

The bandit gang was just setting camp near a stand of junipers and a lush meadow, when I decided we'd come far enough. I'd wait for the sun to set before moving closer. The bandit gang soon had a cooking fire blazing, a beacon that could be seen for miles.

"Okay, Paint, I'm going to leave you here for a spell. I'll be back soon," I whispered. I wondered how much

Paint understood? Not much, but maybe my voice soothed him. I felt a similar connection with Mukue, the bay mustang. I ground-hitched Paint and began to move stealthily toward the camp. Taabe sensed my stealth and followed cautiously. Wolves were smart that way.

I began to hear the songs of the night. The howls of coyotes, hoots of owls, and croaks of frogs filled the air. I began my approach toward the bandit camp. They were caught up in cooking dinner. They had no mind for setting sentries. One man rode horseback among the cattle and oxen while another tethered the stolen horses on a string. He quickly returned to camp.

I was downwind. They'd set their camp near a stand of junipers. Between my own stealthiness, the sounds of the night, and their own raucousness, they'd be unable to hear me. I was well-camouflaged against the trees and was able to creep within seventy-or-so feet of the camp. It was easy to count. There were six in the camp. Adding the rider settling the beeves and oxen, that added up to seven men. It was hard to see their weapons, but I surmised that they were well-armed. I made out a few carbines leaning against a log close to their cooking fire.

"Git one of them there oxen, Jed," called out one man. "Damn beasts be slowin' us down." He laughed heartily. "We be feastin' on one this night." He laughed again and raised what appeared to be a whiskey bottle in the air. Whiskey? That accounted for a strange odor that wafted toward me. The bandits were so confident, they'd decided it was safe to celebrate by feasting and drinking.

I was outnumbered seven to one, but they'd eventually be drunk. I began to seriously consider disrupting their revels. I'd have to wait for them to get good and drunk. Assuming I could rout the bandit gang, I'd be faced with the challenge of herding the livestock back to the wagon train single-handed. I had to be plum crazy! Yet, here I was, and opportunity was presenting itself.

I prayed that God would guide me through this.

Taabe slinked over to me and nudged my arm. "You want to help?" I whispered. Again, I assumed animals could understand my words. I reckoned that Taabe could wreak a bit of havoc among the drunken bandits, especially as they began to fall asleep in their drunken stupor. Taabe licked my arm. "You hungry, Taabe?"

By now, the bandit settling the livestock had ridden in to join the festivities. He didn't want to miss out. I sure enough wasn't going to walk into their midst. I settled back to wait for the whiskey to do its job.

I didn't have long to wait. Once they were asleep, I calmly strode into the camp and took all of their rifles and any sidearms I could find. I stashed them behind a tree a good distance away from the camp. Next, I unhitched the bandit horses and sent them on their way. These tasks done, I stood at the edge of the camp. What to do about the seven bodies snoring away around the dying embers of the fire? Was there any point in waking them? I chuckled to myself. Taabe looked at me expectantly. "No," I whispered. I swear I heard a reluctant sigh, but he obeyed.

Off we went to fetch Paint. I was praising God for my good fortune, when circumstances took an abrupt turn. One of the bandits had to answer nature's call. He was staggering toward me. I froze.

He stopped about five feet in front of me and unfastened his pants. He had yet to look up.

I slipped my Bowie knife from its sheath. If he saw me, I would have to react instantaneously. I couldn't have him making any sound of alarm.

The bandit finished. As he was about to turn back to

camp, he caught sight of Taabe moving in the moonlit night. He was about to call out. I had no choice. I couldn't permit him to rouse the others. I took one step and had my knife to his throat before he could utter a sound. "Do not try anything," I cautioned him.

The bandit reached for the gun that wasn't in his holster. Had he been sober, he might have spelled trouble.

I increased the pressure of my knife against his throat. "If you want to live, make no sound."

Beads of sweat formed on the man's brow, as I pulled him along with me to where I'd ground-hitched Paint. Once there, I hog-tied and gagged him. He'd be no further trouble. I leaned him against a tree trunk. All the while, he looked at me through rheumy, fear-laden eyes. That knife could have quite an effect on some folks, especially when it had been pressed against a person's neck. I looked up at the moon. It looked to be a couple of hours before midnight. My efforts had been downright efficient.

Now, it was time to begin the biggest challenge of the evening. There were a half dozen horses, a similar number of cattle—cows actually, and a dozen oxen. I needed to single-handedly bring the livestock together and move them eastward to the Oregon Trail. With any luck, I'd reach the wagon train by late afternoon. I hung high hopes on the bandits being unable to retrieve their cayuses. If they managed to become mounted, they'd surely come after me. The same oxen that had slowed them would be delaying my travels.

While I had helped my pa a bit, driving small cattle herds on the family's Texas ranch and had rounded up and captured wild mustangs, I was a tenderfoot so far as driving the mixed herd of livestock. Thank the Lord, we reached the Oregon Trail more quickly than I'd expected, and the trail made moving the herd a tad easier. I suppose it had something to do with the way the trail had been cleared and worn over the years enough to form natural passageways through the roughest sections. The most difficult part of this exercise was slowing the cattle and horses enough to keep pace with the oxen.

So far, this had been far too easy. I was not what folks called a pessimist, but I was a bit leery of excessive good fortune. I kept saying little prayers. I shared my concerns with Paint and Taabe as we moved the herd. They likely hadn't a clue as to what I was worried about, but when I wasn't gathering stragglers and strays, I kept a watch on Paint's ears and Taabe's protective instincts.

As the trail paralleled the North Platte River, the smell of water made driving the herd even more challenging. I finally relented and allowed the stock to drink. I regretted it.

I turned to find four men charging at me on bedraggled horses. I assumed these were the members of the gang that had been able to retrieve their horses. What utter idiots. By virtue of taking back the livestock without killing any of them, I'd given them a new lease on life. It seemed that their outright greed and shame at having been outfoxed overrode any common sense. I grabbed my Spencer carbine and spun Paint to face the onrushing bandits.

Pa had taught me that it's not the fastest shooter who wins, but the one who is most accurate. "Lord, forgive me for what I'm about to do," I prayed. I took my time fixing a bead on the first rider. He'd just brought his own rifle up into firing position, when my bullet plowed into his chest and lifted him from his saddle. A bullet whizzed over my head. I shifted to my left, aimed carefully, and brought down a second bandit. The others had just about figured out my range, when they realized that the odds were shifting against them. They spun their horses and beat a hasty retreat.

"Thank you, Lord," I uttered upon realizing that I'd fended off the attackers. In addition to their other sins, cowardice apparently ranked high in the character of the two escaping bandits. Then again, they'd been smart enough to recognize a losing proposition. It was obvious that they weren't returning for their *compadre's* bodies. I looked at Taabe. He didn't seem interested in the two dead bandits soaking up Wyoming sun. Time was wasting.

There was silence but for some snorts from Paint and low growls from Taabe coupled with some mooing and intermittent bellowing from the cattle and oxen. I looked up. The sun was pretty much at its highest. By my reckoning, we'd reach the wagon train in about three hours. First, I had to get the livestock out of the river. Handling the task on my own took longer than expected, but I eventually managed to get the herd once again moving eastward. Hopefully, I'd be forgiven for leaving the two dead bandits to scavengers.

As I thought back on the events beginning last night until now, it occurred to me that not a soul would believe what I'd done. It had surely been God's doing, because I wasn't up to such shenanigans. Had the bandits not gotten drunk, I'd have had to return to the ranch, gather a posse, and put folks at considerable risk. My gambit had been risky, but worked to near perfection.

The time passed quickly enough, and I was soon within sight of the still-circled wagon train. It appeared as though they'd acquired some oxen, but not enough far as I could tell.

Jordan spotted me first. Even from a distance, I could see his jaw drop with amazement. Settlers began to emerge from the wagons. They stared in wonder at the man in buckskins herding their livestock toward them.

Donovan saw me, leaped into his saddle, and rode out to help escort me and the herd. As he approached, a broad grin broke out across his chin. "Dang boss, what took you so long?" He belly-laughed.

I smiled with deep satisfaction. I'd fought the bandits and—surely with God's help—had won. "Just couldn't get these oxen to move faster, Chester." I returned the humor.

"I can hardly wait to hear the story," Donovan replied.

Jordan soon joined us. "How?" he sputtered.

"Tell you in a bit. Let's get this livestock to the wagon circle," I responded. Actually, I simply sat my saddle with a satisfied smile while Donovan and Jordan herded the livestock. I was right pleased to see the last of the rumps of those slow-footed oxen. I followed the last ox into the circle.

Folks were excited. I didn't dare dismount for fear of being crushed by their well-wishing. Jordan rode up beside me. "I don't know how you did it, Mr. O'Toole, but we're grateful."

I had to nearly shout to be heard over the crowd. "I've got to get home to my wife, Mr. Jordan. I'll return in the morning and tell y'all how." With that, I nudged Paint through the settlers and headed him south at a canter.

Donovan stayed back partly to help the settlers, and graciously, to let my return to Morning Star be more private.

* * *

Morning Star stood in the doorway with Moses in her arms, as I approached our house. Concern was writ large on her face. She looked beautiful.

The very sight of her got my heart racing. I reined in and slid from the saddle. I nearly landed on Taabe in my haste. I managed to avoid tripping over the poor wolf and rushed to embrace my loved ones.

At this point, Morning Star had no idea that I'd retrieved the livestock and delivered them to the wagon train. "You take long time. I begin to worry," she lamented. "What next?" she asked earnestly between kisses.

I stepped back. "Nothing," I responded with a shrug.

"Nothing?!" she exclaimed.

"I took the livestock back from the seven bandits and returned them to the wagon train."

Morning Star gave a look of disbelief. "Tell true, Isa O'Toole!"

"Let's go inside, and I'll tell you how it happened." I wrapped an arm around her and Moses and guided them into our house.

She sat Moses in a corner with some toys and sat next to me on the bench alongside our kitchen table. "Tell me true," she said.

"I caught up with the bandits at dusk. They were confident and posted no sentries. They celebrated by getting drunk and passing out or falling asleep. Under the light of the moon and stars, I collected their weapons, turned their horses loose, and drove off the stolen herd." I didn't tell her about the unlucky bandit I had to hogtie or having battled four of the bandits as I neared the wagon train. "God was surely on my side."

"Awentia happy you back," she cooed, and placed her hand gently on my arm.

I reckoned by her voice that we'd be cuddling closely this night. I looked into her eyes. "I love you," I responded.

She laid her head against my shoulder, then pushed away. "Isa hungry?" She meant hungry for dinner.

"Later," I replied. Moses had fallen asleep, and a warming fire called to us from the fireplace.

* * *

I stepped from our house next morning into a crisp, sunny day and headed to the corral. The skies were as bright a blue as I could ever remember seeing. Mukue awaited me. The big bay mustang was especially frisky. I gave him a sugar cube, but it apparently wasn't enough. He nudged me with his nose. At that, I realized he wanted me on his back. I grabbed a handful of mane and swung myself up onto him. He nodded a couple of times. Instead of the usual few tentative steps, he turned and trotted off with me clinging to him for dear life. He picked up his pace, and we were soon racing across the pasture with the wind in our faces. It was sheer joy for me. Now came the test, as I pulled back on his mane. He slowed and came to a halt. I patted his neck, and he whinnied happily. I would never forget this moment of bonding. I gently but firmly pulled his mane to the left, and Mukue responded by turning in that direction. I pressed my legs against his sides, chucked to him, and he began a brisk walk. I leaned forward a little and pressed my legs harder. He began to canter.

I expect that we spent at least an hour out in that pasture getting to understand each other at this next level of our relationship. I still wasn't of a mind to saddle him, but it wouldn't be long. I was committed to preserving his spirit, and we simply weren't ready for bit and saddle.

I pulled up to the corral and was greeted by Donovan.

"The settlers are fixin' to share a feast with you, boss," he said.

I was the reluctant hero. "I suppose I'll have to," I replied.

Donovan nodded. "I'm looking forward to the story, too."

"I was lucky, Chester. God surely was watching over me." I gave him a sly, secretive look. "I didn't tell Awentia, but I had to fight off a couple of the bandits a few miles west of the wagon train. Had to kill two of them. You'll understand better, when I tell the whole story." I gave Mukue another sugar cube and watched as he galloped away. "I suppose I'd better tell Awentia about the invite."

"I think they're going to head out tomorrow, boss. The wounded have returned from Fort Laramie, and they're going to join up with another wagon train." Donovan grinned sheepishly. "Those settlers are some kind of grateful, boss."

The implication was that I'd be embarrassed by their gratitude. I wasn't seeking their praises. I'd simply done what I thought was right, when the opportunity had presented itself. After all, our work, as I saw it, was a reflection of my faith toward fulfilling a purpose. I reckoned that I had no choice but to satisfy their well wishes, as the wagons would soon be rolling westward toward fulfilling the settlers' dreams.

# Chapter 7

# Texas Musings

Morning Star and I enjoyed times like this morning, when we could sit on a bench behind our house and soak up the warming rays of the sun while sipping the best coffee on God's earth.

"Isa no tell Awentia about fight." Morning Star laid gently accusatory eyes on me. She hadn't brought it up last night after we'd enjoyed a great meal with the settlers at the wagon train.

"I didn't want to alarm you." It was a lame reason.

"Awentia count coups...kill warriors...fight Arapaho," she reminded me.

"I'm sorry. I just hadn't seen the point in alarming you." In my sharing the story of retrieving the settlers' livestock, I'd forgotten myself and told the gathered assemblage about the bandits charging at me and having had to kill two of them. Too late, I realized that Morning Star was unaware of that part of my story. I'd been deceptive by virtue of the omission. It was no better than a lie. She had sat there listening with a curious expression, as though she'd been hurt. I'd missed it.

"Isa strong...Awentia strong...we together. Your fight, my fight." She stretched up and kissed me. "Awentia forgive."

I took a long sip of coffee. I sure did love this woman. A little irritation enters our lives now and again. My pa told me that a little irritation can produce good results. By way of example, he shared how irritation causes the oyster to produce a beautiful pearl. Maybe I was Morning Star's pearl.

"Isa still think about Texas?" she asked, breaking my trance.

I nodded. "Now and then.

"We do next year," she said decisively.

"I'd love to sell our horses at a town called Bandera. Cowboys flock to it like bears to fishing." I looked off into the meadows where our horses were romping in the lush grasses. "I'm of a mind to give my pa one of our Quarter Horses. He had a fine mount, but it got old and put to pasture."

"How we buy ranch?" Morning Star didn't mince her words. She got right to a key point in establishing a ranch in Texas.

With that, I pulled a pouch from my vest pocket and spilled the contents into my hand. There sat seven gold nuggets.

Morning Star's jaw dropped. "Where Isa get these?"

"I know a place at a creek west of here. It must be our secret place."

"There's more?" she asked.

I put the nuggets back into the pouch. "A little. It's enough to stake us to a ranch in Texas and some beeves." I calmly took a sip of coffee and put my arm around her. "Meanwhile, we'll make our living breeding Quarter Horses." My mind was beginning to toss about with consideration of the milder winters in Texas. Oh, and there was far less snow. No sooner had we taken final sips of our coffee, when Mukue appeared seemingly out of nowhere.

Morning Star stood. She reached into her pocket, drew out a sugar cube, and extended her hand to the big bay.

Mukue eased on over to us. He nuzzled my hand and found it empty. It took barely a second for him to discover the sweet treat Morning Star was offering.

Morning Star stroked Mukue's nose. It was really the first time that she'd sought to connect with him.

Mukue nuzzled her. I suspect he picked up my scent on her, so she became a trusted friend.

It occurred to me that I'd been a bit selfish with the mustang stallion, though part of it was the long time it took to establish trust. I was pleased that Morning Star was now in Mukue's circle.

We had quite a few newborn foals to look forward to, come next spring. Colts frolicked in the meadows, and we had some two-year-olds that'd be ready for some cowboy yearning for a great horse under his saddle.

Paint was getting on in years, and I'd actually begun to consider putting a saddle on Mukue. The wild bay mustang and I had developed a deep bond. I held hopes of luring him into our horse barn come winter's blizzards.

Morning Star nudged me. "Mukue talk to Isa," she said with a nod toward the stallion. "He say, Awentia ride me," she added with a laugh.

It had never occurred to me. Our Texas musings were still on my mind.

Morning Star was a head shorter than me, and Mukue was a very big horse. I stroked his neck while using my free hand to offer a boost for her. Despite her growing belly, she climbed onto his back in a mere heartbeat. "You look beautiful with him," I observed sort of wistfully.

She smiled and grabbed a handful of mane. They were soon prancing around the yard. Mukue must have sensed that she was with child, as he strode with a gentleness. He wasn't going to subject her to the muscle-stretching daredevilish strides he'd shared with me, galloping across the pasture.

Morning Star's smiles were well worth this interlude.

Donovan rode in from the south pastures with a big grin spread across his lips.

* * *

"Saw Taabe out there a ways," he offered.

I helped Morning Star from Mukue's broad back. "What's he up to, Chester?" I asked.

Donovan climbed down from his horse. "I think he's in love."

"I thought we were enough," I said with a chuckle.

"I could swear that he smiled when he realized I'd spotted him." Said Donovan.

"Guess he needs a mate. You ever consider that?" I'd never questioned Donovan about any interest in women, though I sensed that he'd been with a few.

"Haven't found one that I felt worthy enough to court, boss. I'm just a retired trooper turned cowboy to a passel of horses. I don't own anything. What do I have to offer?"

While I'd never pursued the subject, Donovan had never opened up about it before now. I realized that we might be insensitive to his hopes and dreams. I looked imploringly to Morning Star for help on the subject.

She patted Mukue on his rump, sending him happily off to the meadows and his beloved mares. She smiled at me.

I increased the intensity of my imploring expression.

"Texas," she responded simply.

I gave a questioning look, then I got it. I turned back to Donovan.

"You've been a good hand, Chester. You're loyal to the bone."

Donovan squirmed a little with the uncertainty of what might be coming next. Was I about to fire him?

"We're thinking it's nearing time to set up our Texas cattle operations. Somebody must be in charge here while we do that." Morning Star and I exchanged glances. She nodded. "We'd like to leave you in charge. You've learned the breeding process and could use the extra money and responsibility. Reckon we could carve out a couple of acres up in the northeast corner by the river and build you a cabin."

Surprise and joy seemed to spread like a sunrise across Donovan's face. Not ever in his life had anyone presented such an opportunity.

"And..." I looked off at the Laramie Mountains and back at Donovan. He was hanging on whatever words were to come. "And, we'll take you in as a partner in that six hundred acres spread between us and the Freeman spread. Of course, we'll have to hire a couple of hands." Implied was that he'd need a woman to complete the picture.

"I...I...I don't hardly know what to say, boss. This is like some dream." He couldn't hold back as tears of joy and gratitude welled in his eyes.

"You want to sleep on our offer?" I suggested.

"Nope," he replied with a grin while wiping sniffles from his nose and tears from his cheeks. "I do accept. I'm humbly grateful, boss."

"That'll be partner soon enough, Chester." I shook his hand to seal the deal. A man's word was his bond in this rough frontier part of the nation.

Donovan headed to the barn with a bit of a spring to his step.

* * *

Morning Star gazed at me with pride in her eyes. Here we were, a Lakota woman and half-Comanche man settled in a White man's world. "Isa think on his people?

"Oh, I think about pa and ma," I replied, as we headed inside to whip up some late breakfast.

"Awentia mean Comanche people, the *numunuu,* as you say."

"I do wonder about them. They are on a reservation in the place they call Oklahoma. Maybe we can visit there on our way to Texas." As I said it, I thought on what a long journey that was going to be. While I looked forward to the lands my pa had gifted us at our wedding, the full realization still seemed a long way off.

Morning Star went to the kitchen and stoked the stove. We'd be enjoying eggs with bacon and biscuits. "We visit reservation," she assured me. "Isa kind to Chester," she observed.

"He's a good man. Maybe he'll find a good woman." I could only hope. If the ranch wasn't enough to fulfill the man, perhaps a woman would help.

# Chapter 8

# Saddle Broke

It seemed as though the land was crawling with animal life. We awakened every day to the sweet aromas of the wild. Aspen, juniper, cottonwoods, grasses, sage, and more thrived. There were still small herds of buffalo, wild horses roamed free, and elk herds clustered here and there. Big horn sheep deftly negotiated the cliffs and crevices of the mountains. There was no shortage of prey for the mountain lions, bears, and wolves that God created to keep the numbers of grass-eaters under control. The meat-eaters preferred easy prey like aging buffalo or their calves and sick or wounded prey. Now and then, a rancher might lose livestock, but it was the exception given the overabundance of wild hoofed beasts.

Winter was at our doorstep, or, more accurately, barn doors. We had a lot of horses by now, along with the small herd of a half-dozen cattle. Donovan and I spent plenty of time saddle-breaking the two-year-olds. I wondered whether Mukue was ready to enjoy the shelter of our barns from time to time. If he did, would it afford an opportunity to saddle break him? Would he be ready?

I was mucking stalls in the stable, when Donovan approached.

"If it's all right, I was thinking on heading out to Cheyenne," he proposed. "We're near ready for winter, and I have some things to tend to. Might inquire about hiring ranch hands for next year, too."

Donovan aroused my suspicions. I couldn't help but think that a woman might be involved. I held my tongue on that matter. "I think we have everything under control here, Chester. Go take a few days and see what you can dig up."

"Much obliged, boss...er, partner," he said with a catch in his voice.

"Awentia will fix you up with anything you need."

* * *

I took a longer-than-usual ride on Mukue. The total experience of feeling him under me and the wind in my face was an elixir of sorts. I thought back to when I'd first seen him on the return journey from Cheyenne after selling our first-bred Quarter Horses. He'd ridden himself into my very soul. Now, he'd become a part of me. I almost preferred no saddle between me and Mukue. However, with a saddle, we could venture out longer distances. He'd still be free to mate with our Quarter Horse mares and running with his own mustang mares when on the Laramie Cross Breed Ranch. I suppose that I was rationalizing the idea in a manner of speaking.

I'd had Donovan purchase a new saddle on a trip to Fort Laramie. I didn't figure to use the same saddle that I used with Paint. Now, I tossed it up over the top corral rail and let Mukue have a gander at it. As I saw it, the bigger challenge was going to be the bridle.

The handsome bay trotted up to me. It was a crisp early fall morning. The leaves had just begun to turn. When they did, they'd lend a swath of color to the landscape. Mukue trusted me, and I dared not break it. The bridle? The saddle? Did he trust me enough?

He sniffed at the new object capturing his senses.

Morning Star strolled out to join me. She held Moses on her hip and approached Mukue. She touched his hand to Mukue's nose. "Horse. *Kobe. Sunkawaka,*" she said softly, mixing English, Comanche, and Lakota. It was a touching scene.

I took Moses from her and sat him up on Mukue's back. Our baby son laughed with sheer joy.

The bay? He was nonplussed; sort of tolerating the little bundle on his back.

Morning Star was gently caressing Mukue's nose and forehead, and he was loving her touch.

I found myself a bit envious until it occurred to me that the big stallion seemed to recognize that Morning Star, Moses, and I were as one. That led to another thought. Would he accept the bridle if Morning Star slipped it on? It was worth a try. I eased Moses from the bay's back and set him beside a corral post next to Taabe. Our baby delighted in the softness of the wolf's fur. The entire scene was a collection of senses. I hoped they wouldn't overwhelm Mukue.

"Try to put the bridle on Mukue," I urged Morning Star and handed it to her.

She nodded. Morning Star had bridled her own mare many times, but this would be special. She held the bridle to Mukue's snout.

The big bay stallion snorted and turned his head. He paused as though thinking on the bridle.

Morning Star put the bridle aside. "Wait. I be back in minute." She headed into our house and emerged in but a moment with a Lakota braided halter in hand. It had been stored away in a sack that held memorabilia. "We try this." She held it to Mukue's nose, then deftly slipped it onto his head.

Mukue snorted and bobbed his head before nuzzling Morning Star and accepting a sugar cube from my outstretched hand.

"Do you think he's ready for the saddle?" I mused.

"Ride with halter. He get used to it. Bridle and saddle soon," suggested Morning Star.

With that, I stroked his neck and climbed up onto his back with the halter rope in hand. They'd been braided from buffalo hide. Perhaps, it was the familiarity of the buffalo smell that helped Mukue accept the halter as opposed to the bridle. Or, it might have been that the halter had no bit. Either way, I now had something besides a handful of mane to guide him. It was a first step. I gently pulled his head to the left, and he turned. "It's working," I said to Morning Star.

She smiled and lifted Moses to her hip. "I go inside. Mukue happy, Isa happy," she said with a smile. "God good to us."

Taabe, his babysitting duty completed, trotted off. We watched as he strode up to a female standing off a hundred yards or so away from us. He went to nuzzling and wrestling with her. Donovan had mentioned that he'd seen Taabe with another wolf, so this female must be his new mate. It was reassuring, as wolves were known to mate for life. When Mua was killed, it might have spelled the end for any future mate for Taabe.

I dismounted and slipped the halter from Mukue. As I took a couple of steps toward the barn, Taabe and the female approached me.

I squatted and gave Taabe a hug. He obviously loved it, as I ruffled the fur on his neck.

The female paused, then approached tentatively.

Taabe yipped and redoubled his lovefest with me.

She slunk over with her ears back and took a sniff of my boot. I held my hand inches from her nose. She stared at my hand, as she tried to decide whether to permit me to touch her. I guessed her to be a year or two younger than Taabe. Her color was similar. Finally, she touched her nose to my outstretched hand. After a long sniff, she backed away and trotted off. Now, her ears were erect, and she strutted a bit as though having accomplished some great feat.

"She'll get used to me, Taabe," I assured him. The key was trust. I'd long ago learned that earning and keeping trust were essential. By similar token, I'd been warned to always trust but verify when it came to unfamiliar people. Like Taabe, I chose to size folks up carefully before letting them get close. It had been a beginning. Taabe gave a yip and ran off with her.

* * *

Mukue and I galloped across the meadows several times over the next few days. He had accepted the halter, and I was able to use it to great effect. However, the time was nearing for the next step.

Early November had arrived. We'd already had a

couple of dustings of snow, but nothing serious. There was no early blizzard like last year. I reckoned that the time had finally arrived for bridle and saddle. I hoped he'd handle the bit. I was sitting on a bench in the barn fiddling with the tack, when an idea hit me like a bolt from the blue. I headed back to the house. "Awentia, I have an idea. May I take the halter apart?" I knew it was a sort of keepsake and dared not take it apart without her permission.

She gave me a curious look.

"I plan to attach the bit to the halter. Mukue's familiar with the halter, so the addition of the bit will be less alarming for him."

Morning Star smiled. "Is good, Isa. Awentia come see."

I went back to the barn and modified the halter. It wasn't a half-bad-looking rig. By the time I'd finished it, Mukue was waiting expectantly beside the corral for his daily ride. I think he sensed something new was about to happen, when I gave him an extra sugar cube.

Mukue sniffed at the saddle I'd thrown atop the corral rail, then took a long look at the modified halter I held in my hand.

Morning Star stood watching admiringly while a smiling baby Moses clung to her leg.

I didn't waste any time. I stroked him a few times and slipped the bridle over his head with the bit in his mouth.

Mukue paused and looked at me as if to ask *what do you think you're doing*? He shook his head. I offered another sugar cube. He couldn't resist. I stroked him lovingly, and he settled down. He chewed on the bit a little.

It would have been easy to take a ride bareback, but I

decided to push my advantage. He'd accommodated the bridle. Now came the saddle. I flung the saddle blanket over his back. He didn't flinch. Maybe his acceptance was the very strength of his spirit coupled with his trust in me. I gave him a sniff of the saddle and settled it over his back. Again, he didn't balk or shy away. I fastened the cinch. So far, so good. I took a look over at Morning Star.

She nodded and put her hands together as though praying.

I gave Mukue's neck a couple of more strokes, then placed my foot in the stirrup and climbed aboard. I pressed my knees into his sides. He didn't move. I patted his neck. "It's all right, Mukue," I urged as persuasively as I could manage. I chucked the reins a little and made a clucking noise. That did the trick. He took a few halting steps. I pulled the reins to turn him, and we walked toward the pasture. I could see that he was getting used to the feel of the bit and saddle. "Let's run!" I exclaimed, pressing my knees harder into his sides. He sprang forward faster than a rattler can strike. We ran like a strong wind across the pasture and didn't stop until I pulled him up near the row of cottonwoods that marked the boundary of our ranch.

We rode easy-like back to the ranch. Mukue's head was high. From his back and the energy in his gait, he'd lost none of his spirit. If anything, my strong *sunipu* had seemingly merged with his very essence.

Morning Star was waiting for us. With nary a word, I could tell that she, too, saw the way Mukue and I had bonded as only a man and his horse can.

I rode up to her.

Mukue took a sugar cube from her hand. The bit hadn't bothered his appetite for treats.

I reckon it wouldn't be fair to say that the big bay mustang had been saddle-broken. *Broken* was really not the right word. It implied destruction of spirit, and that certainly was not the case. It was more like saddle accommodation or harmonization.

## Chapter 9

## Trouble

Donovan returned from his sojourn in Cheyenne with good news. The livestock market was burgeoning, the Union Pacific Railroad was going strong, and cowboys were available for hire thanks to cattle drives. He noted that he'd met several cowpokes from Texas who said that cattle ranches in Texas were flourishing. Just as importantly, there was strong interest in great Quarter Horses. Little could light a cowboy's fire like talk of a great horse under his saddle.

"You got a saddle on him?" exclaimed Donovan, when I told him the news.

"Yes. And he rode strong as ever," I noted. "Any other news?" I pressed.

Donovan picked up on my implication. "Maybe," he parried. He managed a sly sort of grin.

Back when we'd sold our first few Quarter Horses in Cheyenne, I'd seen him talking with a woman. I couldn't help but notice at the time that it lifted his spirits, but I hadn't pushed him for what might be happening. I reckoned he'd tell me, when he was good and ready. In any case, I didn't press for more. "Well, tomorrow morning I'm fixing to ride up to that place they call The Emigrant's Washtub."

"That's on the Oregon Trail, isn't it?" asked Donovan as if to confirm what he already knew.

I nodded and continued. "I heard from George Freeman that some fellow named Charles Guernsey was looking to establish a cattle ranch up there. If he's bringing in cattle, that will mean cowboys, and they'll be needing Quarter Horses. I'm fixing to meet him. You're welcome to ride along."

* * *

Donovan and I set out after breakfast. We didn't have an especially long ride ahead. I rode Paint. The old boy seemed friskier than normal, as though he was trying to convince me that he wasn't ready to be traded in for that handsome bay running around our spread.

Taabe was off with his new mate, so wasn't running with us per his usual habit.

The Emigrant's Washtub was situated picturesquely along the North Platte River. The area around featured hilly terrain that hinted at the mountains soon to face travelers. The place had gotten its name from settlers pausing along the Oregon Trail before launching into the rugged lands ahead toward the hoped-for answers to their dreams and prayers.

As to the trail we made, it was as challenging as it was beautiful. Poplar, birch, and some lodgepole pine dotted the landscape along with aspen, cottonwood, and juniper. We'd ride along on a smooth grassy meadow only to find it dive into a deep crevice overgrown with grasses and sage while featuring all manner of logs and rocks. We crossed one creek swollen thanks to a dam built by beaver. They'd warn their kin by slapping their tails on the water. We'd ride into a gorge with red and gray rock formations on either side, only to emerge into a vast vista with the Laramie Mountains as a distant backdrop. Little wonder that game was abundant. Deer, moose, elk, buffalo, and pronghorn were pretty-much most anyplace we looked. I reckon this kept the mountain lions, bears, and wolves well-fed, along with the scavengers that followed them. While Mukue had his modest herd of mares, there were plenty of wild horses running free along the Laramie River. The trail was sometimes tough enough that we walked our horses. We crossed a couple of fast-flowing creeks, flowing a bit more wildly thanks to fall rains.

Cutting northward, we reached the North Platte. We now found ourselves following the Oregon Trail. It afforded far easier travel. We didn't talk a whole lot, as we mostly had to ride single file.

As the trail widened, Donovan rode up beside me. "You think this Guernsey fellow will buy our stock?" he asked, as our horses danced around rocks strewn across our path.

"If he hopes to build a successful ranch, he'll need great cowboys who'll need great horses. I reckon that we ought to be able to strike up a deal." I hoped I didn't sound overconfident. I appreciated that Donovan's military service had blessed him with pragmatism. It was a sobering quality but handy. If he indeed was courting a woman in Cheyenne, I expected she'd appreciate such a solid footing in a man.

"We going to start building that cabin?" Donovan asked.

"We'll get it up before first blizzard, Chester. Don't you be worrying."

"I'm reckoning to make one more trip to Cheyenne," he informed me.

I chuckled. "We'll get it done." Maybe, I thought. It was getting right close to winter's storms. Worst case, Donovan could make do with the humble bunkhouse near our barn.

* * *

The Emigrant's Washtub soon came into view. It was busy to say the least, as two wagon trains had decided to plant themselves there and wait out the winter. They might have been smarter to have camped near Fort Laramie. They'd been overly optimistic to begin with. I expect lots of folks need to actually see the foothills of the mountains before they'll believe the weather and terrain advice folks give them. They dared not be bound by snowdrifts like the ill-fated Donner party, thirty years before that resorted to cannibalism to survive the winter.

Some enterprising trader had set up camp with three wagons loaded with supplies the settlers would need to endure the harsh Wyoming winter. Just north of the river, a house was nearing completion. Intuitively, I figured that to belong to Charles Guernsey. I didn't feature a man from back east necessarily spending a winter in a tent. Plenty of men did but hadn't the resources Guernsey apparently was blessed with.

Donovan and I rode straight on into what appeared to be a center of activity between the two wagon encirclements. A few settlers waved greetings, but most continued on with whatever business they were tied to.

We politely returned waves with the customary touches to our hat brims.

I reckoned that the trader would know the lay of the land so headed his way. He'd set up a lean-to affair to protect against harsh weather. What wasn't stored in his wagons was piled on makeshift tables and shelves under the lean-to.

As we approached, the trader completed making change for a customer and looked up to greet us. "Howdy. How kin I help yuh fine gents today?"

Donovan and I dismounted and shook the kinks from our legs. "I'm Isa O'Toole, and this is my partner, Chester Donovan. We own ranches nearby." I extended my hand.

There was a touch of disappointment in the trader's expression, as he realized we wouldn't be customers. "I be Buzzard Smith, late of Denver," he said by way of introduction. We shook hands. "Kin I help you?"

"I'm looking for a fellow name of Charles Guernsey."

His eyes widened. "Oh, yuh be lookin' fer the fella what buildin' thet thar cabin yonder," he informed me. "Nice fella."

I appreciated the added assessment of Guernsey as being nice. "Thanks kindly." I scanned the man's merchandise. "You fixing to establish a store here?"

Smith smiled. "Mebbe next year."

"We'll stay in touch. Having a place close by for supplies would be right handy." Donovan and I mounted up. "Let me know if you need help. I'm at the Laramie Cross Breed Ranch."

"Whoa!" exclaimed Smith. "Yuh the folks be breedin' them fine Quarter Hosses?"

I turned Paint to face Smith. "That's us."

Smith smiled broadly. "Guernsey'd be a fool to not buy yer hosses."

I tipped my hat, and we rode on toward the cabin Guernsey was building.

* * *

"Sounds like you're getting a reputation," he observed.

"Praise the Lord that it's a good one," I responded with a slight blush. I did need to learn to accept compliments without feeling embarrassed. It was a matter of having pride as opposed to being prideful. I didn't have to boast about the quality of the horses we were breeding, as their fine breeding spoke loudly. With that on my mind, I looked up to see a man who looked to be in charge. We dismounted a few feet from him. He finally looked up from something he was reading. "Pardon me, we're looking for a Mr. Charles Guernsey," I ventured.

The man looked at me with a nasty sneer. "He ain't around. Don't talk with no stinkin' breeds anyhow."

Donovan took an aggressive step forward. "I ain't a breed, mister, so watch your tongue."

The man glared at me, then at Donovan. "No matter. Yer ridin' with one."

I grabbed Donovan's elbow. "No matter, Chester. We'll find Guernsey." I was close enough to the man that I picked up the smell of alcohol. The man was drunk at midday. I wondered whether Guernsey knew? We remounted and headed toward the gathering between the circles of wagon trains.

Upon arrival, we climbed down from our saddles and noted that a man was talking with a cluster of folks sitting on logs. He had an air of command about him. His tailored gray wool suit enhanced an image of accomplishment and polish. From his accent, we could tell that he was an easterner. As we approached his audience, he paused. "May I help you, gentlemen?"

Given the intensity of his presentation, I hadn't expected a greeting. "Er…yes. I'm looking for Mr. Charles Guernsey."

"Well, son, you've found him. To whom do I have the pleasure of speaking?"

George had told me that he felt a political side to Guernsey, and I'd confirmed it right away. "I'm Isa O'Toole, and this is Chester Donovan. I own the Laramie Cross Breed Ranch, a few miles southwest of here. We raise the finest Quarter Horses in Wyoming…maybe all the west." I was gilding the lily, as some say.

Guernsey turned to his audience with a broad, satisfying smile. "See folks, you can make a life out here in this fine territory."

We watched Guernsey regale his audience for a few more minutes before he wrapped up and turned to us. "Pardon, gents. I figure that if I'm going to settle here, it would be handy for a town to spring up. The Union Pacific is nearby, and I expect they could be persuaded to establish a depot here."

I liked that Guernsey was inclined to think ahead. He seemed to have a handle on what it would take to build and maintain a thriving community. As for me, it'd be downright convenient getting my supplies from here compared to running off to Cheyenne. "Are you really going to build a ranch out here?" I asked.

"That's my intention, Mr. O'Toole," he replied. "Come on over to the house I'm building," he invited, as he began to walk toward the construction.

We sort of tagged along behind him. "We stopped at

the house you're having built, Mr. Guernsey. Looks right nice," I said by way of compliment.

"Then you must have met Syd Booker. He's cantankerous but knows how to build a house." Guernsey recognized that his man wasn't the most pleasant gent on the planet. "Hope he didn't offend."

Donovan and I exchanged glances.

"You're raising Quarter Horses, eh?" continued Geurnsey.

"Only the finest. We breed them with mustangs to give them extra agility and toughness," I responded.

We arrived at the house.

The insufferably dour expression on Booker's face was no surprise, given the way he treated us earlier. He glanced at Guernsey as though questioning that he'd have to deal with me, a lower than life itself half-breed.

"Syd, get these fine gentlemen some coffee," were the first words from Guernsey as he approached Booker.

I was sure Booker would refuse, but he grumbled something intelligible and ambled off to the coffee pot.

The house was pretty far along, and Guernsey took pleasure in giving us a tour while Booker fetched the brew. By the time we'd finished our walkaround and sat at a makeshift table, Booker had two steaming cups of coffee set before us and another for Guernsey.

"These gentlemen are looking to sell me their special breed of Quarter Horses for my cowboys. How about that, Syd?"

Syd scowled. "I be happy tuh build yer house, Mr. Guernsey, but I take no truck with breeds."

"Excuse me," responded a surprised Guernsey.

"Yuh heard me…sir!" said Booker, with emphasis on *sir*.

I wanted to step in but reckoned it was best to let the

ranch owner handle his own trouble. I could see that Donovan wasn't very pleased and itched to give Booker more than a piece of his mind.

"I believe you owe our guests an apology. I'll have no such prejudices displayed around here," advised Guernsey.

Booker's face contorted, as he struggled with apologizing. "I...I'm sorry," he finally spat out. "I got work tuh git to." He began to turn and walk away.

"Mr. Booker," I called. "What do you have against folks of mixed races"

The man froze.

Guernsey looked at me as though wondering why I wished to open that Pandora's box.

Booker spun around and gave me a hard look. "My ma and pa be kilt by Kiowa. Any man with Injun blood is evil."

"My ma isn't evil, Mr. Booker. Neither am I so far as I can tell. Evil exists with every people. It's mostly folks filled with envy and greed; people that are angry and full of hatred owing to their own misery. Wouldn't you agree?" I tried to project an image of peace and earnest interest in the man's pain.

Booker had just been challenged by a seventeen-year-old. He didn't like it any. It threw his thinking off. He realized that his job was on the line. Guernsey would take no truck with anyone defying him. "Well...er...guess it be makin' sense."

Guernsey seemed relieved. This was more than a matter of principle. He wanted no interruption with the construction of his home.

"I gotta git back tuh the buildin', boss," said Booker, as he twisted uncomfortably in his seat.

Guernsey glanced at me and nodded.

Booker gave me a *this isn't finished* look and headed out to direct roof construction.

"Sorry about that," lamented Guernsey.

"I've dealt with it," I replied. "Some folks aren't able to conquer their prejudices."

"Hope he gives you no trouble, Mr. Guernsey," offered Donovan.

Guernsey shrugged. "Don't think so." He turned to me. "So, you raise Quarter Horses. I must say that you've grabbed my interest," said Guernsey.

"Cowboys who've bought them seem to want more. Chester here tells me that the word in Cheyenne is that Laramie Cross Breed Ranch Quarter Horses are the best. And I've just mated Quarter Horse mares with a handsome, spirited mustang stallion. Those will be ready in a couple of years." I could see that I had Guernsey's rapt attention for the moment.

"You've intrigued me, Mr. O'Toole. When this place is operational, I'll be sure to send my cowboys over to you." He pulled out a pocket watch and glanced at it. "Oh my, I have some folks to meet with. Please excuse me."

"Much obliged for you meeting with us, Mr. Guernsey," I said by way of gratitude.

With that, he shook our hands and dashed off.

"That went well," I said to Donovan after Guernsey had disappeared from sight..

"Yeah, but that Booker fellow concerns me," he conjectured. "Could be trouble."

I agreed but figured to give Booker the benefit of the doubt for now. The man was carrying some heavy baggage from his past, and it had affected his thinking.

* * *

We didn't reckon to hang around The Emigrant's Washtub for long. The mission had been accomplished, and there were chores to tend to back at the ranch. We finished our coffee, mounted up, and headed out. I looked back at Guernsey's house construction and saw Booker standing among the roof supports and watching our departure. His look gave me a chill. Donovan's concerns made sense.

We alternately rode and walked the trail toward the place from which we'd head south toward the ranch. We were in no hurry, so traveled easy.

We were about ready to leave the Oregon Trail, when a rattlesnake spooked Paint. He reared a mite and nearly dumped me from the saddle. I wasn't sure where the shot came from, but just as he reared, a bullet plowed through Paint's head. I jumped clear of the saddle to avoid him falling on me. Donovan dove from his saddle and grabbed his rifle. We both dropped low and scanned the area.

"Shot came from back there," said Donovan, pointing behind us. "If Paint hadn't reared, it would have got you," he added.

I glanced at my dearly beloved horse. He laid still and wasn't breathing. Mercifully, he hadn't suffered.

There was no sign of the shooter. We waited several minutes, but there were no more shots fired. Maybe, the bushwhacker thought he'd gotten me and left.

I managed to free my tack from Paint. Fortunately, we were only a couple of hours from the ranch. I threw my saddle up behind Donovan and led the way on foot. It didn't make sense to add my couple of hundred pounds of body weight to Donovan's cayuse. Thankfully, I wore boots that were well broken-in, so blisters wouldn't be a problem. But I had much more to be grateful for. If the rattler hadn't spooked Paint, I might have been killed. God's work? Could be.

"Who do you think?" asked Donovan.

"That one of those rhetorical questions, Chester," I replied. "I expect we know."

"Do we go back?" he continued.

I thought on it a moment. With one horse, it wasn't so convenient, plus we weren't positive that Booker had shot at me. I chuckled, much to Donovan's surprise. "We'll let him wonder whether he got me."

Donovan gave me a questioning look.

"Reckon to work on the man's mind a bit. It'll gnaw at him. Did he get me? Was he seen? He'll be looking over his shoulder, fearing revenge every minute of every day."

"Maybe," suggested Donovan. "But, he might be so caught up in his hate that he doesn't care," suggested Donovan.

I hadn't considered that. Evil could possess folks in many ways. Booker might very well be beyond caring. "Let's give it a few days to percolate."

* * *

"Paint killed!" exclaimed Morning Star. Tears filled her eyes, as she buried her face in my chest. "Why? Who?"

"Don't know," I replied. "Sit." I pointed to the bench at the kitchen table. Once sitting together, I locked on to her eyes. Dang, but she had deep, dark, beautiful eyes. They nearly distracted me from what I was going to say. "We had a good meeting with Mr. Guernsey at The Emigrant's Washtub." I paused and took a deep breath. "There was trouble, too. A fellow who worked for Guernsey was prejudiced against Indians, and he let us know. We think he shot Paint."

"He bad man," lamented Morning Star.

"Paint was spooked by a rattlesnake and reared just as the shot was fired. Donovan and I think the bullet was meant for me."

A look of horror initially spread across her face, but it was quickly displaced by anger at what had nearly happened to her husband. "What we do?"

"We're going to give it a few days. I figure the man's curiosity will drive him to investigate the scene. He'll discover that he got my horse and then begin to worry about whether we'll come looking for him."

"We in danger here?" she asked.

I shook my head. "I don't think so. The man is a coward. He might even have run away."

"Awentia see much *wiiya*." She used the Lakota word for danger.

"We'll be careful," I assured her. I gave her a hug just as Moses cried out to let us know he was awake. It occurred to me that we lived a life of contrasts. Here I was sitting comfortably in my house with my family. Only hours ago, I'd been shot at on the trail by some bushwhacker. Living on the frontier seemed filled with such contradictions.

# Chapter 10

## Mukue's Time

When Mukue came trotting in from the meadow behind our house, I think he sensed that something had changed. I suspect it might have been a consequence of the way I stood or the tears welled up in the corners of my eyes at the loss of Paint. He approached me with no hesitation and placed his great head upon my shoulder. Okay, he's only a horse, but I truly believe he was comforting me.

He stood while his custom bridle was slipped over his head and didn't even flinch when the blanket and saddle were affixed on his back. I stroked his neck and hugged him. "It's you and me, Mukue," I said gently.

He turned his head such that I could feel him watch my back as I mounted him. We stood for a moment, then I led him slowly away toward the meadow. I held him to a walk at first, then it seemed time to run. On my silent command, Mukue sprang into a gallop. We blazed across the grasses, dodging occasional sage bushes and leaping small creeks. Mukue's spirit was on full display. We finally pulled up at the top of a grassy knoll at the southernmost tip of the ranch. The Laramie River meandered eastward before us. I could see the overhang where we'd fought off the Arapaho. Wild horses with flowing manes and tails galloped freely on the opposite shore.

We turned and looked back at the Laramie Cross Breed Ranch. Oh my, but it was beautiful. To me, there was nothing else on God's green earth that compared. I smiled to myself. Yellowstone National Park was incredibly beautiful and filled with God's wonders. But the ranch was close enough in my eyes. I patted Mukue's neck reassuringly. It was Mukue's time.

We rode easy-like back to the ranch. I dismounted at the corral. Now, came the big change from our past rides. I dropped the reins, and he followed me into the stable. I removed the saddle and bridle, then lovingly curried his handsomely beautiful body. At the end, I hugged his neck and gave extra strokes to his forehead and nose. From his eyes, I could see that the spirit that had drawn me to him months ago was unbroken. His spirit had joined with mine.

Mukue looked around his stall. There was plenty of hay and water, but he looked troubled. He wasn't comfortable.

It struck me that the stall was too confining for a horse that had spent years roaming free across the Wyoming landscape. Yet, my desire was that he be here ready to ride when needed. I stood, stroking my chin in deep thought. What might I do short of releasing him? Finally, it came to me. It was a sort of compromise. I opened the stall and led him to the arena section of the barn that had been built for training horses. The area was big enough and featured window-like openings with shutters to shield against winter storms. It gave the illusion of freedom. Would this work? Mukue pranced around, investigating every nook and cranny of the arena. Far as I could tell, this arrangement worked. "What do you think?" I asked.

"I think he likes it," said Donovan. He'd been observing me working this out. "You must be inside his head," he observed. "You sure enough have a connection."

I shrugged then laughed. "Only problem is that this is beside where he mates with the Quarter Horses. I don't want to raise his expectations."

We both laughed.

Mukue looked at us as though wondering what was so funny. He trotted around in a circle before coming over to me and nuzzling my hand. I pulled out a sugar cube. It looked as though horse and man had made an acceptable arrangement.

* * *

After my ride and settling Mukue into his new world, I quietly slipped into the house.

"Mukue in arena?" Morning Star asked without looking up from her beadwork.

How did she know? "It seemed best for him," I replied. I picked up Moses and then held his hands while he took a few staggering steps. He'd be running around soon. "*Ana o'a hi'it.*" I teased an invitation to eat in the Comanche tongue. I planned to cook dinner for us this night. She'd worked hard the past few days despite carrying our child, and it was tiring even for as strong a woman as she was.

She looked up at me from her craft. "Awentia hungry. Eat for two." She laughed at her own pregnancy humor.

I had been determined to cook up a feast. An elk roast would be the centerpiece of a meal that included candied carrots and baked potatoes. The rib roast had been in the oven for a couple of hours, so was nearly ready. Cooking aromas hung throughout our home.

Morning Star returned to her beadwork and left me to my culinary designs. Her intricate artistry with the beaded designs on the buckskin dress belied the physical strengths she possessed. "Mr. Donovan have woman," she spouted out of the clear blue.

"You think so?" I asked.

"Isa no see? He go to Cheyenne. Bring her here."

"He'd better do it before the storms," I said, as I pulled the elk roast from the oven and popped biscuits in. "Almost ready," I advised.

"Donovan woman live in bunkhouse," Morning Star lamented. We hadn't been able to complete the cabin before frosts and early storms.

"We'll be sure to finish his cabin first thing come spring," I assured her. I finished cooking and set the feast on the table. I could see from Morning Star's expression that she was impressed. We had just finished blessing our meal, when there was a knock at our door. "I'll get it," I said.

The sun set earlier these late fall days, so it was dark outside. I took a look through the eyehole I'd drilled into the door for screening visitors. In the dim light, I wasn't able to identify our visitor. "Who goes?" I challenged.

"Boss. It's me. Donovan."

I opened the door. "Sorry. Guess that bushwhacking the other day has me timid as a rabbit in a lion's den."

Donovan stepped in. "I just wanted to let y'all know, that I'm heading to Cheyenne in the morning."

The only wintery weather we'd received thus far had barely dusted us with snow. The only blizzard was a couple of weeks back. In between, we'd been rained upon a few times. Bottom line, the weather had been unseasonably warm. "The trip will take several days, Chester. You sure?"

He nodded vehemently.

I looked over at Morning Star, and she nodded to my questioning gaze. "You care to enjoy some roast elk with us?"

"Thanks. Pleased to," responded Donovan.

I scurried over to the cupboard and grabbed another place setting and some cutlery. Once Donovan was settled and had heaped his plate with delectable vittles, I was unable to hold back my curiosity any longer. "Will there be two of you coming back from Cheyenne?"

Donovan sat silently, chewing for a moment. "Yep."

Morning Star and I laid questioning looks upon him.

"Okay. It's a woman. Her name is Pearl. We'll marry in Cheyenne and hustle back here," responded Donovan.

"She know what it like here?" asked Morning Star.

Donovan laughed. "A heap better than where she's at."

It didn't seem fitting to ask where she was at.

"Y'all will love her," added Donovan.

"Praying the weather holds for you, Chester," I said.

"Gonna take a tad longer coming north, as we'll be bringing her things in a wagon."

The wagon sounded like a commitment on Pearl's part. I couldn't imagine a woman packing her belongings if she didn't intend to establish herself someplace. "Tell Pearl that we'll finish the cabin at the first spark of spring," I assured Donovan.

"Maybe get cowboys to come here in spring. We need two," urged Morning Star.

Donovan nodded. "I'll put the word out."

We chatted the remainder of the meal, then Donovan departed to pack for his trip to Cheyenne. Once I finished cleaning up after the meal, we decided to cuddle by the hearth rather than our bed. Morning Star fed Moses, and we were soon asleep in each other's arms.

* * *

The crystal-blue morning sky gave nary a hint of the frigid temperature. Mukue pranced about and bobbed his head by way of making me well-aware that he was ready to ride. I was of a mind to head over to George's ranch. I hadn't spent any time with him since the Arapaho attack, and I was of a mind to hunt. If George was unavailable, I reckoned to lure Hap or Dred into bagging some game.

Mukue and I were soon cantering toward George's Circled Cross Ranch. The easiest route was due north until we reached the Oregon Trail, then eastward. George's ranch spread out below the Oregon Trail just south of the North Platte River and west of Fort Laramie. Mukue was in great spirits. I steered us clear of where Paint had been killed. I still felt bad about his loss. He'd been a loyal, hard-working horse. I'd been blessed to have Mukue to turn to. The bond between a man and his horse was especially strong on the frontier. My pa had told me that the famed Lewis and Clark Expedition found horses so important that they traded away firearms to obtain them. The man and horse relationship was especially close with cowboys. They sought mounts that were agile, fast, predictable, and trainable. A cowboy didn't need surprises when he was wrangling cattle.

Mukue was a big mustang, which led me to wonder what his lineage might have been. There wasn't a mare near or far that refused his advances, as he was all stallion. He was intelligent and quite agile. Mustangs were known to be hard to train, but that hadn't been the case with Mukue. It hadn't happened overnight, but he accommodated me fairly readily once we got acquainted. I knew that horses descended from those brought by early Spanish explorers, so there was no telling what ancestral blood flowed in their veins.

Once we reached the Oregon Trail, I kept a watchful eye for Syd Booker. We were a long way from The Emigrant's Washtub, but I didn't figure to take any chances. Taabe and his new mate followed at a distance.

George's ranch came into view. There were beeves far as the eye could see, and there must have been a dozen cowboys rounding them up for a drive to Cheyenne and the Union Pacific Railroad. They'd be steaks and roasts for hungry folks in time for holiday festivities. It occurred to me that Christmas was but six weeks off.

We pulled up at the ranch house. Running Waters saw me coming and greeted me with a warm smile. I dismounted and hitched Mukue. I gave him a few strokes on his neck and headed up onto the gallery to hug Running Waters. "Where's George?" I asked.

"Me no good enough?" She laughed. "He behind you," she added.

Sure enough, I turned and found George with his omnipresent smile riding in.

He pulled up and limped over to me with arms outstretched. "Isa, how great to see you!" His bone-crushing handshake was followed by a breath-stopping bear hug. "I see you've made a new friend." He nodded toward Mukue. "He's downright handsome."

I smiled. "The mares love him."

Mukue snorted as though acknowledging my observation.

"What brings you to the Circled Cross this fine morning?" queried George.

"I'm itching to hunt. Wondered whether you might be up for it?"

"You might have picked a colder day," he responded with gentle sarcasm.

I had to admit that it was a tad bone-chilling. I was in such high spirits that I'd not noticed the clouds of frozen breath exhaled from the humans and animals around me. I was comfortable in my bearskin coat, heavy buckskins, gloves, and high-topped moccasins. I thought a moment in the frigidity surrounding me. George was right. We had plenty of food, and it was too cold to hunt unless a person was desperate. "Guess it was an excuse to come visit," I confessed.

"Well, come on in and share our hearth," welcomed George. He paused. "It's warmer in the barn than standing hitched to a rail, so get your cayuse over there first," he admonished.

I stabled Mukue and headed to the house where hot coffee, a warm fire, and good company awaited.

"Awentia is due," observed Running Waters, as Esmeralda offered fresh-baked cookies.

"Should be most any day, but likely closer to Christmas," I responded. "I'd be back at the house, but Awentia saw me getting restless and urged me to go out. So, here I am."

"Well, Running Waters has cooked up some venison stew, and you're welcome to join us," offered George.

"Donovan is headed to Cheyenne. Did you hear that he's gotten himself a woman? I've given him some land, and we're building a cabin for them."

"Married? Chester? That's great news." George placed

a fresh log on the fire. "You found yourself a good man, Isa."

"I'm giving him a share, while we set up the ranch in Texas." I barely got the sentence out, as I'd scalded my throat with hot coffee. I coughed and set the cup aside. "I think I'll let this cool a spell." I took a deep breath. "I'm still worried about that fellow that tried to bushwhack me and killed Paint."

George smiled. "God willing, the man has better sense than to try anything in this cold weather. Does that Guernsey fellow know about your run-in?"

"I doubt he knows," I admitted. "By now, his house is likely completed. No telling where his man has run off to."

"Unless he has a personal grudge, I doubt that he's thinking on you, Isa." George took a drink of hot coffee. The scalding liquid had no effect.

"Paint was a good horse," I said out of clear air. Why? I haven't a clue. Some lingering anger?

"I don't think God would take kindly to seeking revenge for a horse," said George with something between a grin and a frown.

"In a way, Paint's rearing at the rattlesnake saved my life. I should have been the one killed." I expect it troubled me that Paint's death had occurred instead of me. I expect that it rankled me deeper than I cared to admit.

"Well, God apparently didn't see it that way," advised George.

"Stew ready," interrupted Running Waters. She turned to me. "You blessed, Isa. God keep you for purpose."

"She's right, Isa. You are a light for others by virtue of your character. It's God's gift."

What could I say? She and George were right. I

needed to stop beating myself up over the loss of Paint. Besides, it was now Mukue's time.

* * *

After enjoying a belly full of Running Waters' stick-to-the-ribs stew, I bade farewell and headed to the barn to saddle up Mukue.

"Howdy, Isa," greeted Dred. "You been to Fort Laramie lately?"

I smiled and shook my head. "Can't say that I have."

"Some fella there been hollering 'bout killin' half-breeds. He be sayin' there be no place on earth fer them. Boast 'bout killin' one." Dred gave me a knowing look.

"Do I look dead?" I asked sort of rhetorically.

Dred laughed. "I'd still be watchin' yerself, Isa."

"Thanks kindly," I responded. Saddled up, I headed Mukue for home.

# Chapter 11

# Donovan Returns

Timing can be everything during winters in Wyoming. As I pulled into the barn, I heard the sound of creaking leather and groaning wagon wheels, as Donovan pulled up.

The vision of loveliness beside him was bundled up such that only her eyes peeked from her face covering. I say loveliness, because her eyes were indeed right pretty. They sparkled with the light of the afternoon sun.

"This must be Pearl," I said, as I moseyed over to the wagon.

Donovan had already leaped down and run around the wagon to assist her in stepping down. "You be right," he rejoined. "Pearl Donovan, this here is Isa O'Toole."

Pearl gave me a cold-numbed nod.

"Pleased to meet, Pearl. How about coming with me into the house to get warm and meet my wife?"

Pearl needed no persuading.

"Come on in, when you've put the wagon and horses away, Chester." I turned to him and lowered my voice.

"You might light a fire in the bunkhouse, too. I'll be back to help after I introduce Pearl to Awentia."

Donovan nodded and went to work unloading the wagon and unhitching the horses.

I ushered Pearl into the house. "Sweetheart, this is Pearl Donovan, Chester's wife. Reckoned she could warm up in here for a bit."

Pearl unfastened the heavy scarf around her head to reveal a strikingly beautiful woman. She looked to be twenty years old or so, though it was hard to tell. "Thank you," she said and held out her hand to Morning Star.

"I'm going to help Chester. You two get acquainted." With that, I headed out to the barn.

Chester was already putting Pearl's suitcases and satchels into the bunkhouse and had a good fire going in the fireplace. I went to work, taking care of the two horses that had pulled the wagon, plus Donovan's mount that had been tethered behind. We finally rendezvoused in the barn. "Well, she's right pretty, Chester. Glad you found yourself a woman."

Donovan looked directly at me. "To be straight, I have a confession."

I responded with a questioning look.

"Pearl is my stepsister…sort of. I married her to get her away from the life she was leading in Cheyenne. It wasn't pretty, if you catch my drift." He busied himself storing away the harnesses.

"Is that legal, Chester?" I pondered.

"Yep. I made certain."

"Y'all love each other?" I asked.

"That's another story. The short answer is yes." Donovan finished with the harnesses and walked over to me confidential-like. "My father was a vicious, hate-filled man. He near beat my mother to death before she abandoned us. He found another woman and they had Pearl. They never married. My father raised Pearl, but beat her, treated her like a slave, and reckoned to have his way with her as soon as she was old enough. His world was one of hate, greed, and lust. He beat me for no reason until one day I fought back and won. Pearl feared him terribly and ran away just before I did. She hooked up with bad people. We stayed in touch best we could. I finally learned that she was in Cheyenne."

The fact that Pearl's mother had never married her father made her illegitimate in the eyes of the state. "But you're in love?" I pressed.

"I think my staying in touch and earnest efforts to help her brought us closer together. When I was assigned to Fort Laramie, I managed to visit her a few times. I felt that we grew closer together. Still, I was unable to persuade her from the work she was involved with. She wanted to escape it, but was lost. When you offered me the opportunity here at the ranch, I figured it was time to express my feelings for her. Well, here we are."

Donovan didn't once mention Pearl's work, but it wasn't hard to figure out. There were many women on the frontier who wound up in houses of ill repute, especially in boom towns full of miners and hangers-on where there was little opportunity for single women. "Well, we'll love her, Chester. Fear not."

"I never doubted that, boss. Y'all aren't that sort of people." He grinned. "You know what they say about pearls?"

"You mean the irritated oyster produces the pearl?" I replied.

"She's faced plenty of irritation," noted Donovan.

It seemed as though he was right. "We'd better get to the house. They'll think we got lost."

Upon entering the house, I froze at the sight of Pearl. She'd shed the blankets and heavy winter clothing and stood before us in a red satin dress that left nothing to the imagination. I gulped hard.

Morning Star blushed.

Donovan laughed. "Pearl has no frontier clothes. I'm hoping Awentia can whip up some appropriate garb."

"I would be very grateful," said Pearl.

I wanted to say that we'd be grateful, too. "Well, I think we can get that accomplished. Pearl is about Awentia's size. Maybe we have something we can give her," I nodded to Morning Star, who headed for a wardrobe that held several dresses of cotton and of buckskin. I was sure that Pearl would appreciate the comfort of the sort of dress we were accustomed to.

Morning Star held a simple cotton dress up to Pearl to see whether it would fit. Pearl was not nearly so lean as her, but we figured the dress would fit with little or no alteration.

"Much obliged," thanked Donovan. "Can she try it on?"

Morning Star nodded vigorously and motioned Pearl to the bedroom for the sake of privacy.

Pearl soon emerged in a more modest dress. It was a vast improvement. That red satin number had likely served as eye candy in Cheyenne.

"Do you sew?" asked Morning Star.

Pearl nodded. "A little."

"We put you to work," she said with a warm smile.

* * *

Pearl turned out to be a treasure. Whatever her previous employment, there was not a shred of evidence of it, as she reveled in being a wife to Donovan. She had the bunkhouse spruced up in no time, though no self-respecting cowpoke would have tolerated some of the decidedly feminine decorations.

It was right after one particularly brutal blizzard, that Lieutenant Dickerson stopped by on one of his patrols. It had been a couple of years now, since I saved his life by keeping him from freezing to death. He was about to be reassigned to Texas and reckoned to bid farewell.

Dickerson was sipping coffee at our table, while the troopers relaxed in the relative warmth of the barn. "Can't say that I'll miss the winters up here," he observed.

"I recall some cold in Texas, Lieutenant," I replied.

About this time, Pearl found her way up to the house. "That was some storm," she gasped, as she swept in from the blustery cold. Upon seeing Dickerson, she froze, but not from any chill.

Dickerson's mouth dropped. "Why, Miss Dais..." His words trailed off as he realized where he was.

There was a moment of awkward silence.

Pearl blushed, then recovered. "Well, I come to invite y'all to dinner," she said while ignoring Dickerson. "Chester and I have fixed something special. Y'all come down about dinner time." With that, she shot a parting gaze toward Dickerson and headed back to the bunkhouse.

Morning Star had no idea what that had been about, but I caught on right quickly. I supposed these sorts of things might happen, just not so soon.

"Well, I'd better get back to the fort," said Dickerson. "I'll try to stay in touch. I'm eternally grateful to you folks. Perhaps, I'll see y'all when you've got that ranch going in Texas."

Soon, Dickerson was leading his patrol back to Fort Laramie.

"What happen?" asked Morning Star. She'd had the gnawing feeling that she'd missed something. I hadn't shared what Donovan had told me in confidence, so she had no idea what sort of life Pearl had led.

"I'll let Pearl tell you." It was all I could think of to say.

"Maybe, we no go to dinner," whispered Morning Star as she clutched her belly, and a puddle formed beneath her. "Baby come," she announced.

I knew what to do.

* * *

Barely an hour passed before our newborn son lay nestled in Morning Star's loving arms. She was exhausted but not so much that she couldn't coo soft words, caress him, and, of course, feed him. He was an O'Toole, and he was hungry.

"What shall we name him?" I quite naturally asked.

Morning Star gazed lovingly at me, signaling that the name was up to me.

I hadn't given it much thought. I'd been caught up with Mukue, the wolves, and the breeding business, such that my mind had postponed coming up with a name for our newborn. Having given our firstborn a biblical name, I was inclined to stay with that course. "Michael!" I exclaimed. "Michael is the great protector, a leader, the archangel. It's a strong name."

With a peaceful smile and nod, Morning Star closed her eyes and fell asleep.

I lifted Michael from her, wrapped him in a blanket, and held him. I caught his eyes. "Michael," I whispered.

When we didn't show up at the bunkhouse for dinner, the Donovans became concerned. They gave us some grace before trudging through the icy snow up to the house. They knocked, but they received no response. Donovan stepped in and was greeted by the plaintive wail of a newborn.

"Hey Isa!" hollered Donovan.

I emerged from the bedroom. "Shhhh," I said with finger to mouth. "Say hello to Michael," I whispered.

Pearl's jaw dropped. "Oh, but he's beautiful," she said softly. "May I hold him?"

Donovan seemed at a loss for the moment, as he watched Pearl cuddle our newborn son. "Congratulations," he finally blurted. It was awkward but heartfelt. I sensed that Donovan craved a family of his own. Did Pearl? She sure could cuddle lovingly with Michael.

"Awentia is asleep," I advised.

Peral handed Michael back to me. "Well, we'll have to bring dinner up here." She spun about, grabbed Donovan by the arm, and headed back to the bunkhouse.

I laid Michael in the cradleboard. Glancing over at the nearby crib, it seemed that Moses had slept peacefully through the birth of his brother. The days had grown shorter with winter's approach, and it was dusk by the time the Donovans appeared with the feast they'd prepared.

Pearl had even made table decorations as a celebration of her new life. The meal was delicious despite having been transported from the bunkhouse.

As we began to eat, I heard a scratching at our front door. "Excuse me," I apologized and headed to the door.

Taabe and his new mate wanted to come in from the

cold, and I obliged. He leaped on me, and I ruffled his great furry neck. I led him over to meet Michael.

After properly sniffing around to get acquainted, Taabe noticed Pearl. He cocked his head questioningly. The expression that had crossed Pearl's face as Taabe lumbered in had been priceless in its combination of surprise, uncertainty, and fear.

"He's mostly tame," I assured her, though the word *mostly* caught her ears.

"He…he…he's a wolf!" Pearl finally burst out. She drew back, as I led Taabe over to meet her.

Donovan stroked his back and let Taabe lick his hand. "See, Pearl. He won't hurt you."

Pearl nervously held out her hand, tentatively for Taabe to sniff.

Instead of sniffing, he gave her hand a sopping wet lick.

She pulled back.

Donovan and I laughed. "He really likes you," I said.

Just then, Morning Star appeared in the doorway to our bedroom. We'd made just enough noise to wake her. "Join party?" she laughed. For a woman who'd just birthed a child, she looked remarkably rejuvenated after her brief nap. She looked over and saw Michael nestled in the cradleboard and Moses beginning to stir in his crib. "We eat," she added and sat beside me. "Meal look wonderful. Awentia hungry."

We enjoyed a wonderful meal. It seemed that the combination of a new addition to our family, the impromptu moving of the meal from the bunkhouse, and Taabe's visit brought an intimacy that might have otherwise been difficult to conjure up. It was sure different.

Most of all, Donovan's return with Pearl seemed to have brought us all closer.

# Chapter 12

## Bushwhacker

We were in danger of life settling into some sort of normalcy in terms of routines. There was a lot of waiting patiently for spring, when mares were expected to foal. Meanwhile, winter was official, and Christmas had arrived.

Pearl was domesticating right quickly. It was as though some inbred desire revealed itself that had been hidden away these many years owing to her rough circumstances. Being around the O'Tooles apparently brought out her natural homemaking instincts. The Freemans joined us for a huge feast along with Hap and Dred. Having George with us was wonderful, as his strong but gentle and affable presence brought a warmth to the gathering. I personally looked forward to gathering around the hearth after dinner to share stories, and of course, the Christmas story.

Christmas at the O'Toole home wouldn't be right without a surprise. So it was that we'd just sat to dine when a loud knock sounded at our front door. I arose to greet our visitor and had taken but two steps, when the door swung open.

Wally Wallace strode in with a sack over his shoulder and a covering of snow which he immediately shook off like a wet dog after a swim. "Yo-ho-ho, merry Christmas!" he hollered. There he stood, legs akimbo like a jolly white-bearded, buckskin-clad Santa Claus.

Everyone sat momentarily stunned at his entry.

"Wagh! It is merry, ain't it?" he exclaimed and followed with a deep belly laugh.

The room burst into laughter, much to Wally's pleasure.

Pearl looked confused.

"This here is Will Wallace, affectionately called Wally. He's trapped more beaver, shot more critters, and fought more Indians than all of us combined. And he's a great friend."

Wally's eyes sparkled, partly from the contrast of stepping in from the frigid outdoors and partly from his sheer happiness at seeing such a joyous gathering of friends and family. "I see yuh got a new one!" he said with an eye to baby Michael. "And Donovan! Good for you, man!" he exclaimed upon seeing Pearl.

I quickly ran to the bedroom and grabbed a chair for Wally. It seemed we'd be blessed with whatever new adventures the old fellow might share. "Come and join us," I invited, as I plopped the chair beside mine.

Wally set aside his sack and joined our repast.

Our post-dinner gathering around our hearth as led by George was entertaining, informative, and blessed. Wally regaled us with his most recent adventures around Yellowstone National Park and a skirmish or two with some Shoshone and Nez Percé. I shared my story of bonding with Mukue and joy at my growing family.

George topped off the gathering with the story of Christ's birth that we celebrated. His rich voice lent a deeply meaningful impact.

As the gathering began to break up, Wally sprung into action. "Wait! I nearly forgot my sack!" he bellowed as only a mountain man could. With that, he began sharing the riches of his travels. He drew each item from the sack with great flourishes. These were riches as defined by Wally and any of us who'd trekked the rugged frontier and met its people. Wally handed out knives in beaded sheaths, fringed and beaded buckskin dresses, necklaces, blankets, buckskin shirts, and more. The sack was indeed a frontier treasure trove.

Finally, it seemed that everything had been distributed around the gathering. I stood watching with the joy felt when folks received surprise gifts. "Wagh!" he hollered. "Seems to be one more in here!"

With great drama, Wally dug deep into the bag and rummaged about. "Ah, what could this be?" he teased. Ever-so-slowly, he pulled a Northern Cheyenne tomahawk from the bag. He ceremoniously walked over and handed it to me. Its steel blade was impressive. The tomahawk handle was intricately carved and featured a leather grip. A colorful feather decoration completed the image of a weapon whose artistic beauty thinly disguised its strikingly-savage, death-dealing function.

"It's…it's beautiful, Wally," I sputtered.

He smiled. "Merry Christmas everyone," he concluded. He turned to me with a wink. "I'll spend this evening in yer barn an' be on my way in the morn." He was out the door before anyone could speak.

"Merry Christmas for sure," I added. I scanned the room. George and his family would spend the night here, as traveling in the snowy terrain at night would be foolhardy. Chester and Pearl headed to the bunkhouse after she helped Morning Star clean up a bit. There wasn't much, as every morsel had been consumed.

When all had settled, Morning Star and I bedded the boys and nestled comfortably in our bed.

"Was good Christmas," she said.

I was already asleep.

* * *

Come morning, I gazed out the window. Smoke curled from the bunkhouse fireplace. I saw Wally heading up the trail northward on his old mule. I wasn't sure when or if I'd ever see him again. He sure had epitomized the joy of gift giving. I held hope that we might enjoy another hunt together one day.

I turned back to the rustling about behind me, as George and Running Waters gathered themselves and family for a cold wagon ride home. Hap and Dred had accompanied them on horseback, so would provide an escort. Not that it was a long distance, but there was a lingering worry over Indians despite the cold weather.

"We'll be heading out," said George, as he finished his coffee. He shuddered reflexively at the thought of the couple of hours ahead. "It was a wonderful Christmas, Isa. You're setting a fine example for how to live here on the Wyoming frontier. The commitment you and Awentia share is God worthy."

George had set the standard for building a life here in the Laramie and North Platte Rivers country. I felt that I was pretty much simply trying to emulate him and my pa.

* * *

"They just appeared," insisted Donovan.

Where in tarnation had they come from? Setting before us in the January sun were three longhorns, one a right-handsome brindle. "I don't see any brands."

"It's strange. I came out to take care of the horses and check our livestock, and there they stood."

At our approach, the steers backed off. From what I could make out, they looked to be hungry. "Let's park a bit of hay over yonder, Chester. Can't be letting these strays go hungry." I headed to the barn with Donovan to grab a half bale. "By the way, now that we're partners, you can call me Isa. Guess it's been a tad confusing."

"I sort of still think of you as boss, Isa," said Donovan.

"How's Pearl?" I asked.

"She wishes she'd listened to me years back. She loves the life out here."

"That's great to hear. I do worry about what's yet to come. I hear that the army under General Terry is intent on capturing Sitting Bull when he leaves Canada. No telling how the tribes will react." I thought a moment on what I'd just said, then chuckled. "Actually, it's White settlers that worry me the most. I fear they'll not have so much respect for the land."

"Expect you're right, Isa," agreed Donovan.

"So, we have these three maverick beeves to deal with. With no brands, we could brand them as our own."

"They're a tad lean. We fatten them up; we can sell them to the garrison at Fort Laramie. It'd be like found money." Donovan smiled at the prospect, as he helped me carry hay over near the cattle.

* * *

"Ah tell yuh, I kilt plenty of Injuns!" insisted Booker.

"Don't doubt you," responded the trooper, tipping back his black cavalry hat and sporting an uncomfortable grin. He shifted awkwardly, as though he didn't want to engage the man. He hadn't chosen this table. The drunken sot before him was an interloper.

"Dead Injuns be good Injuns!" pressed Booker. He appeared to be just about ready to fall from his seat. "Livin' ones be no good to my ma an' pa." Booker stared at the trooper through rheumy eyes. "Yuh e'er kilt one?"

"I don't know, sir. I shot at some in a fight," responded the trooper. He scanned the room as though seeking relief from this predicament.

"Kilt me a breed the other day," Booker boasted. He'd spent weeks here at Fort Laramie regaling anyone he could hold captive about his campaign to kill Indians. "They be the wust. White an' Red skins don't mix none. Only thing worse be White an' Black minglin'."

In his peripheral vision, the trooper saw a couple of his trooper friends enter in a swirl of snow dust and head for a table nearby. He felt a bit of relief. "You'll have to pardon me, pard. My friends just arrived." He began to rise and turn away but heard a familiar click of metal. He froze.

Booker gazed up through liquor-reddened eyes, a Colt revolver shaking in his hand.

"Careful, mister. That thing might…"

"Shoot?" asked Booker. "I ain't done with yuh. You an' Injun lover?" he slurred. The liquor was bringing him to an inexorable end.

"No," responded the trooper nervously.

Booker raised the gun and pulled the trigger. The hammer struck an empty chamber.

The troopers who had just entered caught their

fellow trooper's situation. They ambled easy-like over and stood on either side of Booker.

Booker didn't notice them until they picked the gun from his hand, lifted him from the chair, and hustled him out of the saloon. The only decency they showed was to park him on the boardwalk outside the door rather than throw him into the snow. One trooper threw Booker's empty gun after him.

"Thanks," offered the trooper who had been victim to Booker's drunken diatribe. "He's been hanging around the fort for weeks. Command hasn't the heart to chase him away in the cold. First time he's pulled a gun."

* * *

Donovan and I eventually managed to mingle the three foundling steers with the half dozen head we already had. The newcomers were notably leaner. The brindle had a pretty-fair horn spread, so we judged him to be three or four years old. It nevertheless remained a mystery as to where they'd come from. It's a big country, but unlikely that three head would stray for long.

It was an unseasonably warm day, so I reckoned to ride out to the northern reaches of our ranch. I wore a lined buckskin jacket instead of my bearskin coat. The sun reflecting from the snow could wreak havoc with a person's eyes, so I generally kept my head down and gave Mukue his head. I'd fixed my long hair in braids that hung from either side of my head. I wore a heavy felt hat that featured a headband that Morning Star had beaded. I was right comfy. I had my trusty Spencer carbine just in case we spotted some worthy game. I was only figuring to head out the handful of miles to the Oregon

Trail, so honestly didn't expect much luck so far as elk or deer.

I had the strange feeling that I was being watched. The chill that ran up my spine wasn't from the cold. I struggled to look around me more frequently despite the snow glare.

Mukue and I rode along with Taabe and his mate, tailing us at a distance. Suddenly, a shot rang out. It especially startled me when I heard a bullet whiz past my head. This was no hunter's poor aim. I quickly dismounted with my Spencer carbine in hand and moved away from Mukue. I wasn't about to lose another horse to a bushwhacker. Bushwhacker? Was that Booker fellow back?

I moved toward a stand of cottonwoods and hunkered down. Squinting, I scanned in the general direction from which I figured the shot had come. I saw a muzzle flash and heard another shot blast from among some junipers near the south bank of the North Platte River. The bullet didn't come close. Whoever was shooting had set themselves in pretty fair cover but wasn't much of a marksman. I guessed that the shooter was maybe a hundred and fifty to two hundred yards away. Even as mild a day as it was, the fact remained that it was winter and still cold.

"Did I git yuh, Injun?" came a voice from the junipers. "Where yuh at?"

The voice sounded like Syd Booker. It held that telltale tone of hatred that laid heavily in Booker's voice. I didn't respond, hoping he might think he'd gotten me.

It became a waiting game. I didn't move.

"Yuh out thar, Injun?" shouted Booker.

I waited silently, knowing he'd eventually have to

come out and reassure himself that he'd shot another Indian. It was man to man, *mano a mano*. Fortunately, he was about as capable a bushwhacker as he was a man.

Booker took a swig from his whiskey bottle as he emerged from the junipers with his rifle mostly at the ready. I say mostly, because he had the barrel pointed in front but held the weapon rather carelessly. He took cautious step after cautious step, as he headed to where he'd seen me leave Mukue's saddle. Reaching the spot, he looked around. By now, he realized that there was no blood. Despite his boozy condition, it took him but a moment to see my footprints in the snow as they headed toward the cottonwoods. He was perhaps seventy-five feet from me. I could see beads of sweat on his brow and a worried look in his eyes. He swept the cottonwoods with his rifle and took three random shots. One bullet took a chunk of bark from the tree I sat behind, but I didn't move a muscle. "Ah knows yuh be thar!" screamed Booker. He was as edgy as a sheep among wolves. He brought the rifle to his shoulder and pulled the trigger twice. A hollow click at the second trigger squeeze revealed that the rifle was empty.

This was my opportunity. I stood and walked to the edge of the stand of cottonwoods in full sight of Booker. My Spencer was at my shoulder and aimed at his chest. "Drop the rifle and raise your hands," I ordered. I was no lawman but figured it was what one would do when directing someone to surrender.

Booker froze. "You!" he exclaimed. "Yer dead!" He aimed his empty rifle at me. The booze was governing his actions. He pulled the trigger. Nothing. "A ghost!" he gasped in drunken horror.

"Drop the rifle," I demanded.

"Yer alive..." he said, as reality struck him like a sledgehammer. His face reddened. "Yuh heathin' Redskin!" He dropped the useless rifle, dropped to one knee, and pulled a revolver from his waistband.

The blast from the muzzle of my Spencer tore through the crisp mountain air. My aim was unerring.

Booker's gun went flying. Air escaped with a great rush from his lungs as my bullet crushed into his chest. His mouth went wide and his jaw dropped open as he crumpled to the snow.

I cautiously walked up to him and kicked the revolver away.

Booker tried desperately to breathe. He gasped for air. Blood began to spread rapidly around where he lay. He was a dying man. He'd never overcome the hatred that drove him, and here he was dying on a snowy bed in the wilds of Wyoming. "Heathen son..." he managed as his dying words.

Great sadness swept over me. I hadn't wanted to kill the man. Had I a choice? I so yearned to have had a chance to change his prejudiced, hateful ways. I walked over and picked up his revolver. It was loaded. He was aiming to kill me.

I reckoned that he had a horse around somewhere. I found my way to Mukue and headed for the junipers from where Booker had tried to bushwhack me. Booker's cayuse was tethered a few yards back from where he'd stood in ambush. I led the horse out and discovered that Booker had been tracking me. I suspected that caused the sensation I had of being watched.

Now, came the decision of what to do next. I decided that there'd be too many questions at Fort Laramie. I felt as though someone needed to know that the man had met his end. It didn't seem likely he'd be meeting his Maker. It wasn't all that far to The Emigrant's Washtub, so I decided to give the body over to Mr. Guernsey for burial.

# Chapter 13

# Meeting at Emigrant's Washtub

I surely made a sight riding into The Emigrant's Washtub with a body draped over a trailing horse. I reminded myself that towns on the frontier often didn't amount to much. Any cluster of three or more buildings might qualify, especially if a trading post or saloon were involved. The Emigrant's Washtub wasn't a town in the sense of church, schoolhouse, livery stable, and such, and it definitely had no lawman to be found within miles.

Guernsey's house loomed dead ahead. Smoke curled from three chimneys, so I gathered he was at home. Taking the place in, it appeared that Booker had actually done a mighty fair job building it. It was a shame that alcohol and personal demons had shaped his soul to a bitter ending. It was more edifice than house. Guernsey was quite clearly a man of means. It featured at least three rooms and a covered path to the outdoor privy. From what I could make out, gazing at the place from out front, the fireplaces were apparently situated so they'd heat multiple rooms during the winter. I could make out part of a corral that had been built out back and a place where the land had been cleared and leveled for a barn. I wondered whether the barn hadn't been constructed due to a falling out with Booker?

It had grown a tad chillier since my run-in with Booker. I dismounted, shook out my stiff legs, hitched Mukue, and gave him a reassuring pat on his neck. Taking a deep breath, I strode up and knocked on the door.

I heard light footsteps, then the door swung open.

*"Hola!"*

A smiling young Mexican girl stood before me. "Is Mr. Guernsey at home?" I asked. Dang, but she was a right-pretty young girl. I figured her to be younger than Morning Star, which in turn led me to wonder what her role in Guernsey's house might be.

*"Si. Entrar,"* she said, inviting me in. *"Espera aquí,"* she added.

My Spanish, as learned from growing up in Texas, was a bit rusty, but I knew that she wanted me to wait.

Soon enough, Guernsey appeared. He was dressed more like a man of the frontier than the first time we met. "Why, Mr. O'Toole, what brings you here this fine day?"

"I'm afraid its not good news, Mr. Guernsey," I replied. "Your man Booker has met an untimely end. You're the only person I'm aware of that knew him, so reckoned to bring him here for a proper burial."

"Well, let's head out and have a look." He grabbed his coat. "Maria, *hacer café*," he called over his shoulder, as he donned the coat.

I led Guernsey to Booker's body draped over the saddle of his horse.

"Is that a bullet hole?" he asked upon inspection.

"Truth be told. Syd Booker was drunk and tried to

bushwhack me. I tried to capture him, but he went for a gun, so I had to shoot him. My bullet didn't miss."

"That's obvious," observed Guernsey. "Couldn't you have just wounded him?"

Guernsey's comment set me back. "Have you ever faced someone intent on killing you, Mr. Guernsey?"

He shook his head.

"If a bullet's headed your way, you don't get a chance to duck. Even a wounded man can be dangerous. So it is that I've learned that, when you're attacked, you shoot to kill, not to wound."

Guernsey nodded sort of tentatively as though trying to digest that reality. "Well, I expect you can place the body beside the shed out back. I've got a blanket you can wrap him in. Ground being as frozen as it is, it might be a while before he can be buried." He shook his head with dismay. "I knew the man had problems. Shame it came to this."

"I wish I could have helped him," I reflected.

"Come on in for some coffee before you head home," he invited.

I led Booker's horse around behind Guernsey's house and saw the shed. I found a blanket in the shed, eased Booker from the saddle, and wrapped him in it. There he would lay until spring thaw permitted his burial. I headed for the house to enjoy some hot coffee.

Guernsey's study was beautifully outfitted. There must have been a hundred or more books, and the fine furniture was of oak and mahogany. His window overlooked the valley with the icy Laramie River flowing far off in the distance. It was clear that he intended to build a life here.

"That's a fine horse you rode in on, Mr. O'Toole," observed Guernsey, sipping his coffee.

"Mukue? He's all spirit. I'm breeding him with some Quarter Horse mares." The coffee had cooled enough to not scald my throat, so I took a generous sip. "I reckon you for a man that appreciates what a horse means to a cowboy. He's both a companion and a working partner. It's more about relationship than money. This is why we want to breed the very best."

"Didn't you ride a Paint when you visited a while back?" he asked.

I sighed. Maria had just entered to top off our coffee. She seemed like a sweet young girl. "It's a sad story," I responded. I didn't want to mention Paint's violent end with Marie present.

"I have a feeling that Booker was involved," lamented Guernsey.

Maria left the room, so I took a sip of coffee and continued. "When we left here last time, Booker tried to bushwhack us. He missed me but killed Paint." It hurt a tad to think back on that tragedy. "Booker carried a lot of pain, especially against Indians. He didn't think much of himself. I understand they call that low self-esteem. He tried to bury his pain in alcohol, but I guess my presence dredged up bad memories that liquor wouldn't numb him to. He thought he'd killed me and boasted of it to the soldiers at Fort Laramie."

"That's sad indeed," observed Guernsey. He stood and gazed from his window. "I'm bringing in cattle in a couple of months. Expecting a thousand head. I'll be looking forward to those Quarter Horses of yours."

"Have you met George Freeman?" I ventured.

"He that Black fella with the ranch between here and Fort Laramie?" he asked.

"He's been raising beeves up these parts since my pa brought herds up from Texas and has learned some methods for helping the cattle endure the winters," I advised.

"I expect that I'll have to chat with him," he responded.

Maria peeked from the doorway to see whether we needed more coffee. Guernsey waved her off.

"She's attentive," I observed.

"Very," said Guernsey with a knowing wink.

I shifted a little uncomfortably at that but not so Guernsey would notice. "I see you have quite a library." It was my attempt to change the subject.

Guernsey's eyes lit up. "You ever read *The Pathfinder* or *The Leatherstocking Tales*?" he asked excitedly.

I shook my head. "I've read a bit, but not those."

"They were written by a fellow named James Fenimore Cooper. He grew up in Cooperstown. That's where I'm from. His tales inspired me." He took a sip of coffee and chuckled. "Of course, I'm getting a dose of reality now and then to keep my inspired vision of the frontier under control."

I had to laugh at that. "Cooper sounds like someone I might read," I said by way of considered response.

"You married?" asked Guernsey.

I nodded. "My wife is a Miniconjou Lakota. We have two young sons, one a newborn."

"You married an Indian woman? Guess that's common out here." Guernsey arose and went to the bookshelf. "How'd you meet?"

Clearly, Guernsey was delving into my story, and I wasn't fully comfortable with that just yet. I simply wasn't well acquainted enough with the man. "I saved her from Kiowa. Awentia is a fighter. She has killed enemy Indians."

Guernsey's eyebrows raised at mention of her

warrior deeds. He reached up and pulled a book from the shelf he was scanning. "Here, you might enjoy this." He handed me a worn copy of Cooper's *The Deerslayer*. "Get it back to me when you can."

"I've enjoyed getting better acquainted, but I'd best head home. The skies are turning darker, and that spells trouble."

"Blizzard?" asked Guernsey.

"Likely," I responded.

"Well get along then. It's been a pleasure to meet despite the circumstances. We'll try to be sure the critters don't get at Mr. Booker's remains."

Maria escorted me to the front door. *"Vaya con Dios,"* she said in parting.

*"Si, vaya con Dios. Nos vemos en primavera,"* I replied that I'd see her come spring.

Maria smiled at my Spanish. *"En primavera,"* she repeated.

I headed out into the dropping temperature. My buckskin jacket was barely sufficient. Mukue greeted me with an impatient snort but calmed after a few loving strokes. I climbed into the saddle and turned for home. "I expect he'll buy horses come spring, Mukue," I said in his ear, as though overlooking his likely relationship with the young Mexican girl.

All in all, a day that had begun grimly turned out well. I glanced over my shoulder at the gathering dark, roiling clouds. God was announcing a blizzard. Mukue and I reckoned to make it home in plenty of time to enjoy warm shelter.

# Chapter 14

# Foals Aplenty

The last of winter's snowy blasts ushered March in. We anxiously awaited the foaling of our mares to see whether our hopes for even better Quarter Horses would be fulfilled. I was especially looking forward to the foals from Mukue. Those Quarter Horse mares would be a month or so later, which served to test our patience. We were beginning to recognize the differences between foals born of mustang mares with Quarter Horse sires and Quarter Horse mares with mustang sires. The Quarter Horse sires tended to produce the hardiness and adaptability of the mustangs, while the mustang sires seemed to produce offspring with greater speed and strength. It seemed that we were able to give cowboys a choice that met their particular needs. We maintained breeding records with meticulous care, as Burt Wilkins had advised when we first began our operations. Our aim was to build a great reputation among cowboys for delivering consistently excellent Quarter Horses.

Morning Star fidgeted around the house while I did

small tasks around the barn and corral. Even Donovan was anxious, and Pearl seemed to pick up on the tension in the air. The first foals simply couldn't come too soon. Above all, we prayed that they'd be healthy.

Pearl seemed to have been quick to put her less-than-savory past behind her. She was a natural as rancher wives went. She sure wasn't afraid to tackle even the most unpleasant of chores, like cleaning the outhouse, mucking stalls, doing laundry, and household cleaning. These were a far cry from entertaining men in saloons and bawdy houses. She and Chester seemed happy to be cozily ensconced in the bunkhouse for the present.

That sack I carried with its little cache of nuggets had come in handy, though we had to use the gold sparingly. It wouldn't do to arouse folks to some great find. I'd heard about the Black Hills Gold Rush about four years back that produced the rough and tumble town of Deadwood and resultant greed, murder, mayhem, and debauchery. We were able to purchase building materials, household supplies, and more breeding stock. As to breeding stock, I aimed to have enough horses to not only furnish stock to folks like Guernsey but drive a herd to Cheyenne as well.

I cherished the near idyllic landscapes surrounding Laramie Cross Breed Ranch. We were already seeing ranches spring up. Maybe it was the Comanche side of me that made me more sensitive, but I began to see their concern at the seemingly endless onslaught of settlers taking the land. It wasn't just the taking of land. We had taken land for the Laramie Cross Breed Ranch just as George had taken land for his Circled Cross Ranch. It was that range for wildlife was lost. The buffalo herds were thinning out. I'd seen that some tribes were decimated by diseases White men brought, for which they had no resistance or cure. I was especially concerned as to maintaining the balance of the land. Elk, deer, pronghorns, and even the buffalo were kept in balance by predators like the wolf, bear, and mountain lion. I treasured the times I'd found myself watching a mountain lion stalk a bighorn sheep. To marvel at the yellow eyes focused on the sheep down to the telltale twitch at the tip of his tail captured my in rapt attention. The stealth demanded was amazing and the great final leap as he went for the kill seemed without parallel among hunters of the frontier. But above all else, I admired the wild horses running across the vastness of the plains. They represented a freedom many folks sought to obtain but never would.

With spring came foaling. Typical gestation among our mares was ten to eleven months, depending on the age and breed of the mare. We found that the gestation cycle of mustang mares bred to Quarter Horse sires tended to be shorter. I reckoned this was likely due to the demands of the frontier to replenish herds sooner than later. As it was, we didn't expect Mukue's foals to be born until late spring at the earliest.

Foaling kept us busy, often at inconvenient hours of the day or night. We all became experts at ensuring the foaling process went smoothly, as every foal was a valuable addition to our stock. Recognizing that it took roughly two years for them to be ready for sale, it was a labor of love and necessity.

We guarded as best we could against premature births, but dealt with occasional cases that threatened the health of foal or mare like a retained placenta, stress, improper positioning of the foal, and getting the foal to nurse properly. We relied on a combination of what Wilkins had taught us and our ever-growing experience, as there were no horse doctors out here on the frontier. We were blessed that our mares had few difficulties.

I think Mukue was sensitive to what was occurring, as he became increasingly frisky on our daily rides. In his years running wild, he'd no doubt been present at many a foaling. Once a foal was born, it had to be protected from predators. This was a duty he was no longer called to tend to, and I sensed that he missed it.

* * *

Morning Star stared across the table at me as she nursed Michael while sipping coffee. "When we go to Texas?"

The question came out of the blue. I'd spoken of possibly traveling to Texas this summer to begin setting up our cattle ranching. I clung to that, as my vision quest, as guided by God, had gifted me with the ambition to fulfill my destiny. It was a destiny that had become ours. "We could go in the middle of summer. Donovan can watch over the ranch and break in the two new hires we'll need." I'd committed to bringing two ranch hands on board. I couldn't really call them cowboys, as they'd be strictly tending to horses.

She smiled. "We ride?"

There were no railroads completed as yet from here to Texas. One from Denver to Fort Worth had been approved but was a long way from completion. We'd be traveling on horseback with a couple of pack mules. I preferred traveling by horse, as this mode was faster than using a wagon and offered greater options, so far as negotiating difficult terrain. "I reckon we'll ride. We can mount cradleboards behind your saddle."

Morning Star nodded. She would have liked one of the cradleboards to be mounted behind my saddle, but the need for one of us to have the mobility and agility to defend against dangers was a must. It was still very much a wild frontier. She smiled and nodded acceptance. Cradleboards behind her saddle, it would be.

* * *

By the time June drew near a close, we had eighteen Quarter Horse foals prancing around our corrals. Mukue was the proud sire of five of them.

Soon after putting the last roof shingles in place and moving Donovan and his wife into the place, the two new ranch hands arrived to begin wrangling horses and helping with the upcoming breeding season. I wasn't sure they cottoned to the female frills Pearl had decorated the bunkhouse with, but they didn't complain such that we heard them. Curtains with pink flowers were likely a bit much for their image of manliness. Will Cutter and Joe Moon would just have to get used to it.

I was right-pleased with how Donovan went to work training them in the art of horse breeding. I hadn't been certain that Donovan had it in him. I reckoned the fact that he was a partner rather than hired ranch hand likely gave him greater incentive.

Morning Star and I planned to head for Texas the second week of July, so everything looked to be going smoothly. We spent the evening talking about the ranch we'd build in Texas and how it would complement the ranch here in Wyoming. We counted on my pa to help set up the ranch. One of the great benefits of living out here was the freedoms that the frontier afforded us folks who'd chosen to settle here. Perhaps, it was the Comanche in me and Lakota in Morning Star, but we were sensitive to the Indian ways of roaming free across the wilds. They saw the land as a spirit not to be owned. Ours was a life of no boundaries. Like the buffalo, deer, mustangs, and other wildlife, our lives were unbounded. Prairies stretched for miles, and mountains pierced the sky. Yes, we *owned* the Laramie Cross Breed Ranch, and it had boundaries, but it sat amid the freedom that was the frontier.

# Chapter 15

## Indians!

I headed north from the house to give Mukue some exercise and keep my rear end saddle ready for the long ride to Texas. I've ridden this path so often, and there's now a dirt and rock trail where Mukue had beaten down the prairie grass.

Well, we're riding along easy like, when I glance up and see a startling figure off in the distance ahead of us. In fact, there are several folks behind that lead figure. It wasn't long before I could make out an Indian riding in full ceremonial regalia from chief's feathered bonnet to bone breastplate, breechcloth, leggings, moccasins, quiver of arrows, bow, lance, shield…I could go on. It looked to be a Lakota. I drew my Spencer carbine from the saddle scabbard just in case. They didn't look to be hostile, but we never took chances out here on the frontier. It could be a trick. If there weren't so many wrinkles etched in his bronzed face, I'd be much afraid. Nevertheless, I remained wary. It looked as though the head man had a couple of dozen followers, a mix of men and women of all ages. As this apparition grew nearer, I realized that the old man was Morning Star's father, Spotted Elk.

"Wapitiyu Okle!" I smiled broadly and called out his Lakota name, "Wapitiyu Okle!"

The old chief looked up, smiled gamely, and raised his hand. He looked to be very tired. "Isa! Isa O'Toole!" His voice cracked as though the energy to speak was all he could muster.

*"Oyate Lakota! Ana o'a hi'it,"* I welcomed these *numunuu* with a mix of Lakota and Comanche. I waited while Spotted Elk and his ragged entourage closed the gap to my position. Their spirits seemed to have risen upon seeing me. As they drew closer, I was struck by their condition. In addition to trail weariness, they appeared to be hungry. The travois upon which they dragged their worldly possessions were barely hanging together. "Welcome," I said as Spotted Elk came within conversational distance.

Spotted Elk pulled up alongside. His pony was at least three hands smaller than Mukue, such that I found myself looking down on the once proud warrior.

We leaned in and embraced. *"Ana o'a hi'it,"* I repeated with a motion toward the ranch house. "Awentia waits," I added.

Spotted Elk nodded vigorously with a near toothless smile. He twisted to face his people and told them their destination was near.

I knew just enough Lakota to understand that he was inviting his *numunuu* to stay with us. I gave a warm smile, turned Mukue, and led the way to the house.

Spotted Elk rode beside me. He asked whether we had children and was bust-a-button proud, when I answered that we had two boys. He wanted to know if they were riding ponies yet, so I assured him that they would when they grew big enough. He was concerned about whether Morning Star was a good wife. I had no trouble assuring him that she was.

I wanted to ask why he was here and where he'd traveled from, but decided to wait.

* * *

Given the condition of this ragtag Lakota band, the ride to the house was painfully slow. As we drew near, I saw Morning Star walking from the barn. She hadn't seen us just yet. Finally, she looked out in my direction. Upon seeing Spotted Elk, her face came alive. "Ate! Ate!" she called out and began to run toward us.

Spotted Elk mustered the strength to dismount. It was clear that his aging bones ached from his journey. He'd barely gotten his footing, when Morning Star was hugging him.

I heard murmurs and saw smiles coming from the followers of the old chief. The elation was tempered by tiredness. They'd apparently come a long way.

After greeting her father, Morning Star stepped back and saw the bedraggled condition of the band. We exchanged looks.

I brought my fingers to my mouth like I was eating.

About this time, Taabe showed up and managed to create a bit of a stir. His new mate was with him, along with three pups, but the Lakota didn't see him as a friendly interloper. I made a show of hugging and petting Taabe and tossing the pups in an effort to get the band more comfortable with his presence.

Meanwhile, Morning Star said that there was no space for everyone inside our house. She asked her father to have everyone gather between the house and bunkhouse while she went to work pulling together some grub.

Donovan and our new hands strolled up from training colts in the arena and were joined by Pearl as they responded to the commotion.

"Pearl, would you be so kind as to help Awentia. These are Lakota refugees led by her father."

Everyone pitched in without hesitation to do their part in helping the trail-weary travelers.

It wasn't long before the band was chowing down on the food Morning Star and Pearl had managed to pull together on short notice. For the Lakota, it was a feat. The grateful expressions on their faces exclaimed what words could not.

With Morning Star and I planning to head to Texas in just two weeks, we had to figure how we'd handle the crowd that had come upon us. "Do you think they'd be comfortable camping down near the Laramie?" I asked Morning Star. The river seemed appropriate, as they were a proud people, and the north bank of the river was far enough from our house to afford them the illusion of independence. Importantly, it wouldn't disrupt the breeding operations.

"Good place. Awentia ask Wapitiyu Okle," she replied.

It was quickly settled that the band would camp near the river.

I pulled Morning Star off to the side. I knew she was anxious to catch up with her father, but I was intent on knowing what had brought them here.

We invited Spotted Elk and one of the three warriors in the band into our house. Her father was amazed at the creature comforts inside. They were a long way from teepee décor. He quickly discovered Moses and Michael and was overjoyed with their innocent laughs.

Morning Star opened the conversation about how and why they came to us.

Spotted Elk explained that they'd gone off to Canada with Sitting Bull and his mostly Hunkpapa Sioux. He described the first year as being little short of idyllic. There was game aplenty, and the Canadians made no trouble. However, the Canadians began to tire of their presence, especially given incessant pestering from the US government. Learning that Sitting Bull planned to journey back to the United States and turn himself in next year. Spotted Elk and other Miniconjou Lakota decided to depart before Sitting Bull, and despite winter storms or perhaps because of them, managed to avoid being captured by US soldiers. However, their travel wasn't easy. Game was scarce, and disease halved their number. They also battled a small war party of rogue Cheyenne, losing two warriors. Spotted Elk recalled where Crazy Horse had camped with his Oglala Lakota and recalled that it was a place where they wanted to settle. As it turned out, his hunch proved correct, as our ranch wasn't far from where the Oglala Lakota had camped.

* * *

The arrival of Spotted Elk and his small band forced us to reconsider our planned travel to Texas. I dearly wanted to get things staked out near my pa's ranch, while Morning Star's heart was pulled toward caring for her aging father. We had sent a letter to my folks describing our intentions, so I reckoned they anticipated our arrival.

"Wapitiyu Okle has many more summers, Awentia," I advised.

Morning Star sipped her coffee thoughtfully. As she often did, she enjoyed the black brew while nursing Michael. She looked lovingly at our baby son. "It is not easy, Isa," she finally responded. "You will travel faster without me and our sons."

I had to admit that bringing a two-year-old and a newborn would tend to slow us down. The journey would be long and arduous. It had been just the two of us when we traveled to Yellowstone National Park. We faced dangers, but were easily up to the challenges. With the boys in cradleboards and two pack mules, we would be more vulnerable. We'd considered this when making the decision for both of us to travel to Texas. The arrival of Spotted Elk and the condition of the Indians had now given us pause to rethink our plans. Both of us going began to take on the essence of the impetuousness of youth. If I went by myself with a single pack mule, the journey would take a month each way. With Morning Star and our sons, it would take at least six weeks each way...perhaps more. "There's a bigger question we must answer." I was trying to be sensitive to Morning Star's feelings. "Your father's...our people...will surely be discovered. The agency will want them on the reservation."

Morning Star gazed into her coffee. She was torn between the love of her father and her people and the inevitability of their destiny. They would most likely be taken to the Standing Rock Reservation, far to the north of our ranch. Many of Spotted Elk's remaining Lakota wouldn't survive the journey. As soon as a patrol from Fort Laramie discovered the campsite, the word would be passed through command. At best, the band might buy a few weeks of peace camping on the Laramie River before being discovered. Would there be a fight? If there was, it would surely be a massacre. "I will talk with my father. He must know the truth." She was resigned to the fate of her people. Their future, as determined by the US government, may or may not have been right, but it was a reality that had to be faced.

"If a patrol comes by, there could be trouble," I said resignedly.

The presence of the Miniconjou Lakota posed a serious dilemma. "I'll talk with Donovan and the men, so they'll be on the lookout. Maybe, they can turn away any patrols that come near." I feared that Spotted Elk might be desperate enough to take a stand against removal to Standing Rock.

We stared across the table at each other. Finally, Morning Star took Michael to the cradleboard and placed him near his napping brother. She turned quietly. "You must go to Texas."

We did need to get the southern part of our ranching enterprise underway, and it required my personal attention. This life in Wyoming might have no boundaries, but life seemed to place them before us. I pretty much had it figured that mankind might plan, but God was the ultimate arbiter. "It's settled then." We held hands and prayed that all would work out with Spotted Elk and with my journey to Texas.

# Chapter 16

# Texas or Bust

I explained the situation with the Lakota to Donovan and our ranch hands, and they were supportive. I'd be gone for more than two months, and we could only hope and pray that all would go well in my absence.

"I still know a few of the troopers, boss. I can keep them away," advised Donovan. He still called me boss despite now being a partner. I'd nearly forgotten that he'd spent six years with the US Cavalry, including his time at Fort Laramie.

"Much obliged, Chester." I turned to Cutter and Moon. "Any questions? I'll be leaving tomorrow morning and be back by the end of September."

The two hands nodded. They enjoyed the horses and weren't about to jeopardize the opportunity they had here at the Laramie Cross Breed Ranch.

With that, I went to work making final preparations for my journey. I thought about taking a spare horse, but decided that it would add another concern, be tempting for any bandits or Indians, and reduce my adaptability in any tight situations. Mukue and the mule would be sufficient. Also, I figured that Taabe would follow.

* * *

The day for my departure was crystal clear with an azure sky that seemed even bigger than it actually was. Morning Star and I had spent a romantic night and were grateful for Pearl, who'd been good enough to care for Moses and Michael. We'd had the house and our furs before the fireplace fully to ourselves.

Now, it was time to head south. I'd kissed the boys, though only Moses was old enough to truly appreciate his daddy's love. Michael was too young for my absence to be noticed, but I hugged and kissed him anyway. I wondered what our boys felt when nestled in my big arms? What did they sense in looking into my face? I was a giant to them. Try as I might to get on the cabin floor to play with them, I nevertheless towered over them. I looked forward to the day, when we'd go riding and hunt and camp together.

Mukue was excited. By virtue of all my preparations, he surely sensed what laid ahead. I said my goodbyes to Donovan, Pearl, and our ranch hands before a farewell hug and kiss with Morning Star. I mounted up and turned the big bay southward. Our mule gave a protest bray before a gentle yank on the tether got him started behind us. The mule was named Bertrum.

We were about a mile out, when I turned and waved. Morning Star was still standing with our sons. Moses mimicked her wave. It was altogether heartwarming and sad. I'd so wanted to have Morning Star with me on this adventure to Texas. If absence supposedly made a heart grow fonder, I reckoned we'd be extra fond of each other two months from now.

I stopped briefly at Spotted Elk's encampment. I must admit that I was impressed with the resourcefulness of these people. The camp was nestled among the cottonwoods within easy reach of the Laramie River. There was plenty of game around. Morning Star had explained the situation to her father, and the Lakota seemed to accept the inevitable. Whether they still would if confronted remained to be seen.

* * *

The ground I had to cover over the first couple of weeks wasn't especially difficult compared to the mountainous territory to the northwest. The landscape featured broad prairie lands and rolling hills. The mountains were behind and to the west of us. Once south of the Laramie River, my only concern was any rogue Arapaho or Southern Cheyenne hostiles that might lurk about with hearts filled with hatred for the encroaching White settlers. I'd also heard that there were also folks out there —White, Brown, and Black—that wouldn't think twice about helping themselves to what a lone rider with a pack mule might have of value. Humans of many skin colors seemed to have succumbed to sins of various natures. While most folks sought to build lives through honest labor, there were those who sought shortcuts to wealth by taking from them. The frontier was a land of both good and evil opportunity. It took great strength of character to endure against such forces.

Dangers aside, a traveler such as myself could live quite well from the land. I had plenty of coffee stored on old Bertrum, plus an emergency pack in my saddlebags. Morning Star had sent me off with a generous supply of beef, elk, and venison jerky, as well. I appreciated the variety. There were plenty of elk and deer for the taking as needed, plus there were bears and mountain lions if I dared take them on. Perhaps it was the Comanche blood in me, but this was all second nature to me. Living around my folks and then having been on my own at a young age, I was one with the wild. I'd lived out here long enough that I was like one of the animals in the sense that I knew their code of existence. I'd kill what I needed to survive, but no more than that—unless in self-defense.

I had yet to see Taabe. With responsibility to his growing pack of a mate and three pups, I would have been surprised if he'd tailed along. I counted on the abilities of Mukue and Bertrum to sense danger.

As I dug through my cooking supplies on my first night on the trail, I was met with a wonderful surprise. Morning Star had baked some bear sign, my very favorite sweet treat. Naturally, that got me to wishing she was with me. After dining, I'd enjoy the bear sign, then go to sleep with her in my dreams.

* * *

I saw nary a soul during the first week. I crossed the South Platte River with no difficulties. Mukue was ever alert, and Bertrum plodded along dutifully. A few buffalo ventured across my path, and a few deer, elk, and even pronghorn caught my eye. I was sure that predators lurked, but they stayed out of sight. I'd had the sense to bring along the book Guernsey had loaned me. Despite the natural jostling of being on horseback and keeping an eye out for any danger, I managed to begin reading *The Deerslayer*.

I camped about two-days shy of the Arkansas River. The terrain was dry as a bone, but I managed to find a dry creek bed where I could build a small cooking fire shielded from view by the few grasses and shrubs that yet survived. I didn't especially care for the spot, but me and my hard-traveling companions were tired. Despite Mukue's endurance and my alternately walking and riding him, he needed a rest. If I had to call upon his speed, I needed him rested sufficiently to offer it. Bertrum? He seemed tireless.

I decided to conserve water so I passed up coffee. I'd shot a small doe the day before and focused on cooking up the last of it. Naughty me.

Seemingly out of nowhere, a tall, gangly man ran to Mukue and leaped onto his back. Bad move! I'd swear that Mukue jumped at least four feet straight up, humped his back, twisted, and ditched the interloper unceremoniously. The man landed with a sickening thud and caught a hoof that tore a nasty gash in his arm. Just as quickly as the violence ended, Mukue settled to chowing down on the grass as though nothing had happened.

The man lay groaning and moaning with pain. He was bleeding from the nasty gash on his arm and looked to have a busted leg. He was likely lucky not to have a broken neck. I stood with my Spencer carbine in hand. By the law of the frontier, the penalty for stealing a man's horse was death. By that measure, I had every right to put him out of his misery. But. I'm not the sort of man who goes around shooting horse thieves, especially ones that fail miserably.

I walked over to the man. He wore a holster but no

gun resided in it. He'd lost his hat, and his clothes were coated with trail dust and now blood.

"Mercy," he begged. "H…h…help me."

I sensed that the man was on the run from something or someone. "You have a name?"

His breathing was shallow. Maybe he'd broken some ribs, too. "Smitty," he managed to say. "I be hurtin' bad," he managed to get out breathlessly. His face was losing color.

I looked at his leg. It was bent to one side just above the knee and also bleeding. He had what they called a compound fracture, as bone had broken through the skin. Unless I stopped the bleeding, he was going to bleed out right in front of me. I went over to my saddlebags, found a couple of bandanas, and strode back to Smitty. I had begun to tie a bandana over the gash in his arm to stop the bleeding, when I realized that he'd stopped breathing.

There, I sat pretty much at a loss for what to do. I hadn't been gifted with the ability to bring anyone back to life and only knew of one person who had accomplished that feat. I looked up at Mukue. "You done him in, my friend," I said, while trying to decide what to do with this dead body.

There was no way that I figured to haul a dead body with me on the trail ahead. "Dear God, what would you have me do?" I sort of reflexively looked to the heavens to decide what to do with this unanticipated circumstance. Bertrum brayed. Must have been the smell of death in the air. Anyhow, that caused me to look at him and see the small shovel tied to the pack on the ground beside him.

I must say that Smitty tested my sense of smell. With violent death, the victim often voids excrement, and this was no exception. Nevertheless, I rifled his pockets and came up with a folded paper, an engraved watch, and a wallet with some money in it. I unfolded the paper. It featured a likeness of Smitty with a reward for his capture dead or alive. Well, the reward was attractive but I had plenty of money. It wasn't worth me hauling him all the way to Pueblo, the nearest town of any size in these parts and a couple of days from my present location. So the man needed a proper planting, as it wouldn't be right, morally, to leave him to the buzzards and coyotes. I decided that burying him in the stream bed likely wasn't the best idea, as the body would be revealed when water once again flowed. I dug a grave on a bluff overlooking the dry stream bed and interred poor Smitty. I reckoned that I'd eventually mail his personal effects to the sheriff in Pueblo first chance I got.

Well, I hoped this would be the first and last excitement that I'd encounter on the trail.

* * *

Crossing the shallow waters of the Arkansas River was a milestone, as it meant that I was better than a third of the way to my pa's ranch in Texas. Having traipsed this way once when I headed north on my vision quest, I reckoned that I was pretty close to the path I'd traveled. In any case, I felt that I was making great time. Mukue and Bertrum were in great shape, so I permitted myself to feel cautiously optimistic. There were still nearly three weeks ahead of me.

The landscape might be best described as barren. Not much green foliage was to be seen. Thanks mostly to a scarcity of rain, there'd been what folks called a *big dry* in these parts. I occasionally crossed terrain where a prairie fire had passed through and blackened my path. With the sand hills ahead of me, I took advantage of a rare spring to make sure my canteens and bota bags were full.

Texas and Adobe Walls laid about a week ahead of me. It had only been a half-dozen years back that Quanah Parker had led several hundred Comanche in the Second Battle of Adobe Walls in an attempt to punish the buffalo hunters that had broken the Medicine Lodge Treaty of 1867. The attack was fought off, and the Army removed civilians. A fort was rebuilt, but burned out by Indians. A couple of years later, a store was opened near Turkey Track Ranch. All in all, it was a decidedly desolate, sparsely-populated place. I reckoned that I wouldn't feel comfortable until I reached the Canadian River and made my way due south to Palo Duro Canyon.

By this time, I'd finished reading *The Deerslayer,* but decided to read it again since Mukue and Bertrum had no appreciation for my singing voice. It helped pass the time, as I finally reached Coldwater Creek and Texas soil.

# Chapter 17

# Palo Duro Canyon

Call me naïve, as my excited anticipation of Palo Duro Canyon was sorely misplaced. While my *numunuu,* my Comanche forefathers, had mostly abandoned the place for the reservation near Fort Sill in the Oklahoma Territory, the canyon had subsequently become infested with human vermin.

I'd learned from Donovan through his cavalry friends that a mix of Comanche and White traders called the Comancheros ruled trade throughout the Comancheria, comprising much of Texas and eastern New Mexico. Their trading tended to get a bit rough in terms of where trade goods were legitimately and illegitimately obtained. Shortly after the Second Battle of Adobe Walls and the move of most Comanche to the reservation, the Comanchero trade pretty much petered out. They'd established their unofficial headquarters within the depths of the one-hundred-fifty-mile-long Palo Duro Canyon. What remained within the formidable confines of the canyon tended to be mostly undesirables who supported their existence by fair means or foul. Donovan's friends had known very little about the current residents of the canyon. My pa had driven cattle through here. What could go wrong? Thus, I found myself riding blindly into a nest of human rattlesnakes.

Approaching the canyon is an amazing experience. After mile upon mile of flat prairie lands, a traveler suddenly comes upon this vast hole in the ground. A mostly dry stream runs through it, and its walls are a strata of mixed reds and oranges rising hundreds of feet from the canyon floor. Indian blanket and blackfoot daisy lend their blooms to the scene amid buffalograss and sand sage. Wildlife is abundant with plenty of deer, coyotes, bobcats, mountain lions, and reptiles, especially rattlesnakes. The landscape features cottonwood trees, junipers, soapberry, hackberry, mesquite, and willows, which combine to afford plenty of cover for bandits to ambush unwary travelers. So, there I was heading into my potential Armageddon.

* * *

I reckon to have not gone more than four or five miles, when Mukue halted with ears pricked up and nostrils flared. He snorted, and his eyes said that there was danger lurking. Bertrum had the good mule sense to pull up and stay quiet. My trusty Spencer carbine found its way into my hands and sat handy-like across my saddle pommel. My hand went reassuringly to my Colt .45 caliber Peacemaker nestled in its holster on my hip. I was all too well aware that I preferred the rifle over the revolver, but it made sense to have access to both on this journey into dangerous territory. I nervously stroked my bear-claw necklace.

Two men rode out from behind a mesquite tree

ahead of me. They were nasty-looking critters, if ever there were any. From floppy broad-brimmed felt hats to worn-at-the-heels boots, they spelled trouble with a capital *T*. Bandoliers crossed their chests with plenty of ammunition for the Winchesters in their grubby paws. The muzzles pointed in my general direction.

"Howdy, pilgrim. Whar yuh headin'?" said the larger of the two through a scraggy beard.

I simply stared back with a squinty-eyed look as though studying them; which I was. Something caught my eye, and I hoped it might afford me an edge in this confrontation. The man who'd spoken wore a well-worn beaded buckskin shirt of Comanche origin. Could he have tribal roots? "*Kuha*," I finally ventured in the Comanche tongue as a greeting.

"*Kuha*?" he said, obviously surprised.

"*Hee nahii Nuu yee nah?*" asked the second man, inquiring as to whether I was Comanche.

"*Haan*," I responded affirmatively. "*Tate* Buffalo Hump." I told them that my grandfather was Buffalo Hump, whom they'd know as the great war chief of the Penateka Comanche.

"Yuh speak English?" asked the scraggy-bearded man.

"I am Isa O'Toole," I said with a finger to my chest.

The scraggy-beard rubbed his chin thoughtfully. "Yuh know Jack O'Toole?"

I wasn't yet sure whether I should feel relieved. "He's my father."

The two put their heads together and did a bit of whispering with each other. They finally turned back to me. "My handle be Farley DeGrange," said the bearded man. "An' this be Kyle Jones," he said with a head nod toward his companion. "The sun be dippin' kinda low. Yuh figger tuh make camp?"

I wasn't so sure that I wanted company, especially given that I had no idea what these two might be up to. I think they'd initially planned to rob me and possibly worse. Then again, if what I'd shared about my Comanche roots had dissuaded them from foul play, they could become my safe passage through the canyon. "I'd be pleased to share my coffee," I said by way of invitation.

"We got a site o'er yonder," DeGrange informed me. "Yuh got a pipe?"

Any self-respecting person of Indian descent carries a pipe, and I was no exception. I hadn't had use for it in a long time, but it looked as though it would be coming into play. I nodded. "Lead the way." With that, I followed them. They led me to a spring-fed pond a couple of hundred yards beyond the mesquite tree they'd hidden behind to ambush me.

We all dismounted at the campsite. They had a lean-to structure and a fire pit, so it wouldn't be much trouble to brew coffee and fix a meal.

"That be a right fine hoss yuh got," commented DeGrange.

"Mukue? He's a one-man sort of horse. You mess with him, he'll kill you." I hoped to scare any untoward thoughts from DeGrange's mind.

What occurred next could only have been God's work.

"What the!" exclaimed Jones.

Standing not ten feet from the two was Taabe. He studied them just as he might size up prey and then walked over to me and nuzzled my hand. I ruffled his neck friendly-like.

DeGrange and Jones simply stood with slack jaws.

"It be true!" declared DeGrange.

"How's that?" I responded with a smile and knowledge of what was coming.

"Yer family runs with wolves," he uttered, his facial expression a combination of fear and amazement.

"Strong *sunipu*," I assured him. It was strong medicine indeed. "Any idea the power in those jaws. I've seen a deer's leg crushed." I paused for effect. "And Taabe here has killed Arapaho."

Whatever guarded respect my Comanche blood had conjured up in these two had now turned to something approaching reverence. It was as though they believed that I possessed powerful spirits that their minds were unable to wrap around. DeGrange took a long, hard, appraising gander at me. "Where'd yuh git them bear claws?" It was a rhetorical question.

I smiled confidently. "From a bear."

"Told yuh," said Jones to DeGrange.

"Where yuh be comin' from?" asked DeGrange as he went about stoking the fire and gathering vittles.

"I raise horses north of here in Wyoming."

"What brings yuh this way?" he continued.

"Reckon to visit my pa," I answered.

"Spose yuh know there be danger in this here canyon?" queried Jones.

It seemed time to shift the conversation. "Why are y'all holed up here?"

That caught DeGrange off guard. He sighed and took on a more relaxed appearance. "Tradin' ain't workin' out with Comanch gone."

They were a rough-looking pair. "What did y'all do before trading?"

Jones perked up. "I did some wranglin'," he admitted. "Stopped after I busted a leg."

"Aren't there ranches around?" I asked.

DeGrange looked southward. "Fella name of Goodnight be havin' his JA Ranch down thataway," he responded with a nod to the south.

"How come y'all aren't with this Goodnight fellow?" I pressed.

"Had a fight, an' he kicked us out," confessed Jones.

By now, DeGrange had some venison frying and was brewing some of my coffee. "Ah thinks we be jus' 'bout ready to eat." He extended an empty tin plate my way as an invitation.

"Thanks kindly," I said and took the plate. I still didn't trust these two, so vowed to be extra cautious.

We sat around for the next hour swapping stories, though they were mostly these two drifters sharing tales of their lives dealing with the Comancheros. The Comancheros traded in weapons, household goods, foodstuffs, and livestock. The trade goods were not always obtained by legal means, and this led to occasional violence and ill will. The Comancheros were comprised of a mix of mostly Comanche but also indigent Whites looking to make enough profit to subsist. With the last battle at Abobe Walls and the moving of the remnants of the Comanche nation to the reservation life, the trade business essentially dried up.

As we cleaned up after chowing down on what turned out to be a right fine dinner—considering—I stood back and took a long gander at the two. "So, tell me, Farley. You a God-fearing man?"

That seemed to grab DeGrange's attention. He might have noticed that I said a blessing before eating that evening, but nothing had been said. "I reckon...pretty much," he replied lamely.

Knowing that I was now treading on the lands of the JA Ranch gave me pause to reckon that I'd best be on the lookout for Goodnight's ranch hands. It was indeed a grand ranching endeavor that he and his partner, John Adair, had built. I'd never met Charles Goodnight but had heard tales of his near-legendary cattle drives up the Western Trail that my pa had forged. Of course, the sizes of the herds my pa sent north paled in comparison to the huge herds Goodnight drove. I'd also heard that Goodnight was so wed to the outdoors that he never slept inside the magnificent home he built for himself and his wife. He slept on a porch outside their bedroom. In my mind, he was surely a special breed. But that was neither here nor there, so far as Jones and DeGrange were concerned. They'd apparently run afoul of Goodnight, so I wasn't inclined to have them with me were I to run into the rancher. "You might think a tad more on it," I advised.

DeGrange nodded, and the three of us were soon sleeping under a blanket of stars in the depths of Palo Duro Canyon.

# Chapter 18

# Going it Alone

"Yuh say yer headed tuh yer pa's ranch?" asked DeGrange, as we broke camp at the rising of the sun and under a vast blue sky. The wind had picked up a bit, but that was typical of the Texas Panhandle.

"That's my plan," I responded.

"Mind if we tail along?" ventured Jones.

I can't say that I was overjoyed at the prospect of having company on the trail ahead. I'd grown accustomed to setting a steady pace, and these two would likely slow me down. Worse, they might decide to toss their fears and apprehensions aside and waylay me. On the other hand, my pa had taught me to be welcoming so far as possible with folks. "I'm reckoning to be moving right quickly, Kyle. If y'all can keep up and don't have a problem riding through the heart of JA Ranch country, you're welcome to tag along."

They looked at each other. I figured they were seriously weighing the prospect of running into JA Ranch cowboys. DeGrange sighed. "Best we stay clear of the JA," he lamented.

I suppressed a sigh of relief. "Well, I wish you fellows the best of luck."

"Reckon we'll head north to Deadwood. Heah tell there be gold thar," said DeGrange.

"Good luck with that. *Vaya con Dios,*" I said, earnestly wishing them Godspeed. I hadn't the heart to advise them that the gold rush up there was winding down. Actually, it was more than that, as Deadwood and the gold rush had represented the hard breaking of the Fort Laramie Treaty and led to the Plains Indian Wars and the Battle of Little Bighorn. It had been judged by many to be the beginning of the end for the Plains Indians. Nevertheless, I had mixed feelings, as I watched DeGrange and Jones head northward. It's sort of interesting what men choose to do when they see that their expectations continue to be unmet. They were sure-as-shooting wandering into trouble. I hadn't been up near the region they were headed since my brief time with Custer and the Yellowstone Expedition. The two soon faded into the distance. That prickly chill did go up my spine, as I sensed that I'd not seen the last of DeGrange and Jones.

* * *

I decided that traipsing through JA Ranch lands might not be for the best. Chances were that Goodnight was on a trail drive, plus I just might meet more of the likes of DeGrange and Jones. Reluctantly, I wended my way through crevices and canyons, negotiated rocky trails leading ever-upward, and left Palo Duro Canyon behind. I counted my blessings that I'd managed to avoid the serious trouble that might have brewed with DeGrange and Jones. There wasn't much I could do now but pray for their souls.

About now, I was reminded just how sweltering hot Texas could get. Why, I'd bet the chickens were laying hard-boiled eggs. While strong, steady winds were characteristic of the Texas Panhandle, they didn't relieve the heat all that much. It was like blowing hot air around inside an oven. The winds did serve to kick up enough dust to be reminiscent of riding drag on a cattle drive. I recall seeing some of my pa's drovers coming back literally covered in trail dust for having ridden drag. The only skin showing was under their hats and behind their bandanas. Water? My sweat alone could fill buckets.

I headed southeastward after climbing from the canyon. Crossing the Canadian River signaled that I was deep within my ancestral territory. Decades ago, the Comanche ruled the region as nomadic traders. They'd realized that they needed to supplement a diet of buffalo meat with vegetables. They never stayed in one place long enough to plant and harvest crops, so they became traders. What did they trade? In addition to buffalo hides, clothing, blankets, and weapons, they—shamefully—conducted a robust trade in humans. They'd capture folks, enslave them, and trade them for necessary goods. Occasionally, they'd accept a captive into the tribe, as had happened with Cynthia Ann Parker, who married Quahadi Comanche Chief Peta Nocona and were parents of famed Chief Quanah Parker. Quanah Parker had led what became the final gasp of the Comanche, losing at the Second Battle of Adobe Walls.

Given my vision quest and travels from here to Wyoming, I had gained a deeper appreciation for what my pa and ma must feel when looking back at territory they once called home. Ma was especially touched, as she had been daughter to the mighty Chief Buffalo Hump, who was brother to my pa's best friend and blood brother Spirit Talker.

* * *

The countryside was still so wide-open country that I saw nary a soul as Mukue, Bertrum, and I made our way southward. My thoughts frequently strayed to Morning Star. If it was true that absence made the heart grow fonder; well, mine was filling to overflowing. I missed our conversations, our riding together, picnics, sharing time with our sons, and even the less savory ranch chores we shared. I found myself anxious to be home.

I felt more comfortable now that Taabe was with us. It amazed me that he'd found his way to me. The timing of his arrival turned out to be perfect. I still hadn't figured out why God had chosen me to have a wolf companion. He'd done the same for my pa with Zeb. God hadn't chosen a bear or a mountain lion. I reckoned it had something to do with the combination of loyalty, courage, family, and discernment that characterized the life of the wolf. Then, too, wolves enjoyed a life with no boundaries. They were known to travel hundreds of miles across unimaginably rough terrain.

I finally reached the Pedernales River. I struck a solemn mood upon passing where my Comanche grandparents had camped. It was sacred ground for me. It was from this place that Buffalo Hump had led a thousand warriors on his famed march to the sea forty years ago, killing, sacking, and burning as they marched toward the sea. He'd taken the measure of Texans and the Army.

I reached the old Pinta Trail. I'd skirted around Fredericksburg. While I was tempted to stop there and replenish my supplies, I knew that the Rising Cross Ranch was ever-closer. The Pinta Trail hadn't changed much, since back when I'd accompanied my pa on one of his journeys to Fredericksburg.

While water in the creeks was low, it was enough to sustain travelers. The trail offered a pleasant respite from the flatlands that characterized the Texas Panhandle. This was the northern end of what was called the Texas Hill Country.

I did encounter travelers headed north. These brief passages invariably amounted to little more than nods of heads or tips of hats. Texans were not generally a talkative lot, especially to strangers met on wilderness trails. There surely were a wide variety of characters that I rode past. A couple folks seemed to recognize me as a half-breed and looked at me as though wanting to say something disparaging, but held their tongues upon seeing Taabe and the fact that I was well-armed.

I finally reached the Guadalupe River and left the Pinta Trail, turning Mukue close to due east. The Rising Cross Ranch would take less than a day to reach.

Occasionally, I spotted small herds of longhorns grazing, though I more often encountered solitary beeves looking for decent forage. I looked forward to owning my very own cattle. That part of my dream, as manifest on my vision quest, wasn't that far off. I still hadn't decided on what breed I would raise. Hopefully, my pa would help me with that. From what I'd heard, there were plenty of choices. In addition to longhorns, Brahmans, Angus, Herefords, and Shorthorns were popular among western ranchers.

I was sort of daydreaming, when I came upon my pa's favorite fishing spot along the south bank of the Guadalupe River. A pecan tree still shaded the spot.

Gazing into the river water, I spotted silvery flashes of the still-plentiful bass that Pa used to take us to catch on hot summer days. This marked the far western boundary of Rising Cross Ranch, as evidenced by a sign stuck in the ground for that purpose.

I'd been mostly alone this past five weeks, but for Mukue and Bertrum. I sort of wished they could carry on conversations. I did discover that neither of them especially cared for my singing. I'd read *The Deerslayer* three times during my journey. I felt a sort of kinship to Natty Bumppo as the deerslayer, though half of me related to the mighty Mohican Chief Chingachgook. It left me wondering how the landscapes they peopled compared to places like Yellowstone National Park. I reckoned I'd never know, though I'd been taught to never say never.

So, while I was going it alone physically, I had the companionship of my hopes and dreams. I could converse with Mukue and Bertrum with no negative responses; at least none that I could sense. There was that matter of them not cottoning to my singing.

## Chapter 19

## Rising Cross Ranch

I'd changed physically and generally in my presence. I was far more self-assured. In the five years since I left on my vision quest, I'd put plenty of muscle on a frame that had added a couple of inches to my height. Mukue pranced some, as I reckoned he must have felt the anticipation coursing through me. Taabe would occasionally run circles around our tiny caravan.

At the fishing hole, I had reached the far-western boundary of the ranch. A lone rider came into view. Despite the distance, he looked to be my brother Peter. I wasn't certain. Mind you, there was no fence strung as yet. I simply knew that this was the boundary of the Rising Cross Ranch. The little weather-beaten sign that identified the property was merely a convenience for the unknowing.

As I crossed, the rider turned and headed my way. "Where you headed, partner?" came the call. It was Peter. I knew that bass voice. Dang, but he could sing a lick.

"Looking for Rising Cross Ranch," I responded. Mind

you, I was a tad dirtied up from a month on the trail without access to decent bathing or fresh laundry.

Peter pulled up in front of me and took a long, searching stare at me as though sensing something familiar. "Well, you've found...Isa!" he hollered, as recognition swept his face.

Not another word was spoken. We leaped from our saddles and engaged in proper man- hug greetings.

*"Haa marʉ́awe. Ana o'a hi'it,"* he said by way of Comanche greeting.

I laughed. "You bet I'm hungry, brother." I could almost taste my ma's cooking.

We remounted and headed toward the big house.

"I thought you were bringing Awentia. That mule is a sorry substitute," he chided.

"Her ailing father showed up, so she sent me to this Godforsaken part of the earth by my lonesome." I reckoned to return humor for humor. Texans, even brothers, didn't take kindly to insults about their state.

"You looking to set up that ranch you've been dreaming of?" he asked.

I nodded, as we meandered all-too-slowly toward the big house. I desperately yearned to see Ma and Pa.

"That's one fine stallion, Isa," he said, finally saying what had been on his mind since our greeting.

"Mukue? It's a long story. I'll share it after dinner," I teased. Mukue put a little extra energy into his canter as though knowing he was being talked about.

Peter noticed Mukue's spirit despite a month on the trail. "Mukue. Spirit. Good name," he observed.

* * *

We soon found ourselves reined in with the big house staring me in the face. Peter dismounted first and looked to be ready to bound inside and announce my arrival, but I put a finger to my mouth to signal quiet. I motioned to the stable. "Let's just stable our horses," I said, holding back my excitement at having arrived.

Peter nodded mischievously, and we led our horses and Bertrum to the stable. Upon entering, Peter pointed to a vacant stall.

Well, I opened the gate to the stall and found myself eyeball to eyeball with my pa. There was a pregnant silence as though the world had come to a screeching halt. I think it was the first time I'd ever seen tears from my pa. We hugged.

Finally, Peter had enough. "Y'all gonna have an all-day lovefest, or are we going to eat?"

Pa and I turned and pulled him in. "Food can wait," said Pa.

Even Taabe moved into the cluster. Pa reached down as though he'd found a long-lost friend. Zeb had passed away a couple of years back, so Pa missed the companionship of his wolf partner.

We finally broke apart and stood for a moment, simply taking each other in. "Ma will be so happy to see you, son," Pa finally blurted. "Let's wash up and head in."

I did my level best to clean off the dirt and grime of the trail. I yearned to dive into the old swimming hole, but that wasn't to be for now.

We walked leisurely onto the gallery, and Pa entered first. "Totsiyaa? We have visitor."

Blue Flower, my ma, looked radiant as she turned from the stove with a smile to greet the unknown guest. Her jaw dropped. "Isa! Isa!" she cried, as she dropped the frying pan and ran to me. She smothered me in a hug.

I finally freed myself long enough to hold her shoulders and gaze into her loving eyes.

"You…you've grown, Isa. You big man," she said with tears of joy streaming down her cheeks.

It struck how closely she resembled Morning Star. Ma had also been a bit of a warrior woman when she and Pa had been courting. "Awentia sends her love. I'd hoped to bring her and the boys with me, but her father is ailing."

By now, my little sister Nadua had turned. She'd been a mere four years old when I'd departed on my vision quest after the attack on our home by the *pistoleros*. Now, she was a pretty nine-year-old. She'd grow to share her mother's beauty. "Welcome home, Isa," she said as though trying to reconnect from the past.

I finally broke free of my ma and walked over to hug her.

"Let's eat," urged Pa.

We spent the next hour feasting and talking up a storm. My ma's cooking quickly brought me to realize what I'd been missing. Morning Star was a fine cook, and I was pretty fair myself, but my ma was incredibly good. Plus, she'd had consultation with Perez, the cook on our trail drives, who now strictly cooked for the ranch hands in the bunkhouse.

I learned that Pa's sister and her husband had departed to start a dry goods importing business in Galveston. The Amish couple who'd tried to squat on the Rising Cross Ranch years back still lived up the lane and helped Ma and Pa with ranch chores. Overall, the ranch was in good hands.

While I dearly would have liked to have spent at least a couple of weeks here at the Rising Cross Ranch, time was precious in that I truly yearned to be back with

Morning Star. After dinner, we sat around and chatted until well after sunset. Pa had taken up George Freeman's habit of gathering around the hearth after dinner to talk of faith, current events, and whatever was on our minds.

* * *

A couple of days after my arrival, Pa, Peter, and I headed to Bandera to meet with my pa's old friend and business associate, August Klappenbach. He pretty-much knew all that transpired in the cattle business around South Texas.

My pa wanted me to understand who the important players in the cattle game were. Between Goodnight's and Adair's JA Ranch and the nearby King Ranch, were dozens of smaller yet economically vibrant ranches and farms. Bandera had become a hub for the cattle trade, and the several hundred fine citizens were already dubbing it the cattle capital of Texas.

I'd never met Klappenbach, as my pa had begun to obtain supplies from Kerrville after some problems with folks in Bandera over the issue of slavery. Early on, Pa had recruited ranch hands from former troopers from nearby Camp Verde. The Army had been experimenting with camels, and that hadn't set so well with any self-respecting horseman. My pa had run a modest underground railroad, training escaped slaves to be drovers and running them north on cattle drives. There were indeed Black cowboys, so the ruse worked. I suppose it was our friend George Freeman who inspired the idea.

We rode easy-like into Bandera up to the general store, looked around, dismounted, and hitched our horses. Pa hadn't been here in a while, so he wasn't quite certain as to what to expect. We strode into Klappenbach's store. I must say that we were likely an intimidating trio. We were all big men, a couple of inches over six feet tall and carrying plenty of hard-earned muscle.

A young lady behind the counter glanced up. Her jaw dropped. She'd seen plenty of cowboys, but not so big. While Pa and Peter were dressed in traditional cowboy garb, I still wore my buckskins head to toe, even in the stiflingly hot Texas climate.

Pa stepped forward. "Is August around?" he asked gently.

"Mr. Klappenbach?" replied the young lady nervously.

"Not to worry, I'm an old friend," assured Pa. "Tell him Jack O'Toole and his sons are here."

She scurried off toward the back of the store to Klappenbach's office.

August Klappenbach soon emerged with a broad smile. He was a robust-looking man with a ruddy complexion. "Why, Jack O'Toole, how wonderful to see you!" he declared.

"Good to see you, August. These are my two boys, Isa and Peter," he said, motioning to each of us in turn. "Isa's family is in Wyoming. He owns a ranch where he breeds Quarter Horses far superior to anything around these parts. He's of a mind to establish a cattle ranch up near my Rising Cross spread. Peter here will likely be running the family spread one day."

"Well, you've come to the right place, Isa." He gave me a once over and smiled disarmingly. "Looks as though he favors his ma but has your physique, Jack."

I shook off the veiled compliment. Pa had told me that, while Klappenbach was a man of business, he tended to flattery.

"You say you're breeding Quarter Horses. Anything special, son?"

I balked a tad at being called *son* but took it as the man being affectionate. "We're matching them with mustangs for greater agility and endurance. They're in demand and going for top dollar in Cheyenne."

"I suppose you're not figuring to bring them down this way?" pressed Klappenbach.

I shook my head. "The crisp mountain air and lush Wyoming meadows seem to suit them right fine. I'm not sure how they'd fare in Texas. That's why I figure to breed beeves up near my pa's place. I'll be needing some hands and a capable foreman to handle maybe four hundred head to start." I felt my pa's eyes on me. Glancing at him, I caught a faint nod so figured I must be saying the right things.

"You prepared for all the investment in housing, barn, fencing, feed, equipment, and the like?" asked Klappenbach.

I'd been leaning against a table, so took this opportunity to stand. I towered over the man but smiled so as to avoid making him uncomfortable. "I have a pretty fair idea, Mr. Klappenbach." I struck a humble *aw-shucks* pose.

The man chuckled, as he realized I'd grown up on my pa's spread and been operating the Quarter Horse breeding for several years. I obviously knew what it took to run a ranch. "I do have a couple of gentlemen that I'd be pleased to introduce you to. One used to work with Richard King over at the King Ranch and now has a sizable spread himself. In fact, you might hustle your way to the King Ranch. Mr. King has been ailing a bit and giving management duties to a fellow named Robert Kleberg. He's worth a talk, as they developed their own breed called Santa Gertrudis. They're a Brahman and Shorthorn hybrid that are meaty and can stand harsh conditions. Of course, your pa here has done quite well raising cattle." By the time he was finished, Klappenbach was nearly out of breath. Folks in Texas didn't generally tend to be so long-winded.

"I'm much obliged for the advice," I said evenly.

"How about y'all come back in a couple of hours and join me and the missus for dinner?"

"Thanks kindly," responded my pa. "I recall she cooks up a mighty fine dinner."

With that, we left to stable our horses for the night.

I did excuse myself for a bit. I'd brought a couple of those gold nuggets with me from Wyoming, and I needed to turn them into coin. I reckoned that coins would raise far fewer questions than the gold nuggets. I surely wanted no gold rush hitting the Laramie Cross Breed Ranch. The bank wasn't far up the street. I'd carried my treasure this far and expected no problems.

I tipped my hat to a couple of ladies. Women were still vastly outnumbered around these parts. Just before I stepped into the bank, I caught sight of a couple of rough-looking characters leaning against the front of the local watering hole. One in particular seemed to be judging me. My buckskins and braided hair likely caught his attention, but I saw his eyes drop to the Colt Peacemaker holstered on my hip. I stopped for a second and caught his eyes, sending as strong a message of *don't mess with me* as I could muster. He and his companion said something to each other, turned, and entered the saloon. I wished I could read lips. From what I could make of their sneers, whatever they said wasn't exactly kind.

The clerk inside the bank assayed my nuggets and began to count out a stack of coins. "You find Eldorado, young man?" he asked, though he looked at me suspiciously. "I ain't heard of any gold mining around here."

"I got them up north toward Montana Territory." I wasn't about to reveal that they were from my land in Wyoming. The last thing we needed was a bunch of Texans rooting up the pristine beauty of our land.

"You from around here?" The clerk was asking too many questions.

"I grew up north of Bandera. I'm Jack O'Toole's son."

The clerk's eyes widened a tad, and he shut his pie hole. Apparently, my pa was known around town for better or worse. I suspected that his anti-slavery views back during the War Between the States hadn't set well with some folks. A lot of residual ill will hung about.

Well, I finished my banking business and headed back to the stable. The two men who'd been watching me were apparently in the saloon, as the boardwalk in front of the building was free of loiterers.

I reached the stable uneventfully. We'd be cleaning ourselves up best we could before heading to Klappenbach's place for dinner.

* * *

Klappenbach's wife cooked up a delicious dinner and topped it off with scrumptious cherry pie. It was getting near midnight, when we headed to the stable to bed down with our horses. Full stomachs tend to make folks sleepy, and we were no exceptions. As we walked in, we were met by the stable boy...or what was left of him. He'd taken quite a whipping by the cuts and bruises we could see.

"What happened?" asked Pa, as he drew closer to inspect the poor boy's wounds.

"Thet hoss o'er thar," he managed to say. He pointed to the stall that housed Mukue.

I walked over to check on my big bay stallion. He appeared to be fine at first glance, but the stall had taken a beating. There was blood spattered on the walls, but it wasn't Mukue's.

Again, Pa asked, "What happened?"

"Fella, he try tuh take thet bronc. He be havin' none of it. Beat thet fella up right fierce."

"And you?" I asked, joining my pa in examining the poor youngster's wounds.

"I triy tuh calm thet hoss, but he din't take kindly tuh thet," he replied.

"Sorry you had to get hurt. Is there a doctor around? Someone needs to tend to your cuts," I advised.

The boy gave a pained shrug. "I be okay."

While Pa tended as best he could to the boy's injuries, I took a closer look at Mukue. He trembled slightly with uncharacteristic nervousness. He'd been hit with a whip or quirt, but bore no serious physical wounds. He took considerable comfort in me hugging his great neck. "You're okay, Mukue," I said soothingly. "I'm here." Roiling in my head was a desire to find out who'd tried to steal my horse, much less hit him. Horse stealing was still a hanging offense. Mukue finally settled down.

"Somebody's walking around with some nasty wounds, boys," observed my pa. "We'll do a bit of nosing around tomorrow."

* * *

Pa and Peter sacked out on some fresh hay piled in a corner of the stable. Me? I couldn't sleep. Finally, I decided to take a walk.

The full moon and millions of stars seemed to light up the landscape nearly as well as daylight. I stuffed my Colt in my belt as a precaution and strode from the stable. This was still the wild west, so packing a gun was in order. Of course, I never reckoned on having to use it.

I strode past several buildings. The alleys in between were dark, shadowy places that actually gave me a creepy feeling. I'd been to some big towns, but—like Bandera—they led me to an ever-greater appreciation of the wide open spaces where a life knew no boundaries.

I figured I'd walked a hundred yards or so and had begun to think about heading back to the stable, when I heard a groan from an alley. I slipped my hand over the butt of my revolver and paused to listen. I heard the groan again.

I eased over to the corner of the building beside the alley and stared into the shadows. I was barely able to make out the form of a man lying in the dirt. I cautiously stepped into the alley, stopping to let my eyes grow accustomed to the dim light.

The man lying in the darkness of the alley was holding his ribs and struggling to breathe. He gave off another groan. As I came closer, I could see that he was bleeding profusely from a head wound. So far as I could tell, he was unarmed. He'd taken quite a beating. I put my Colt back in my waistband and bent over him to take a closer look. I realized that he was one of the men who'd been sizing me up in front of the saloon when I'd been heading to the bank. I'd figured correctly at the time that he was up to no good.

The man heard me and turned his head toward me. "Oh! No!" he gasped. "An Injun!" Fear leaped from his eyes.

I realized that I was wearing my fringed buckskins

and had braided my long dark hair. In the dimness, I likely looked like an Indian. "Who whipped you so bad?" I naturally asked. About this time, Taabe ambled up alongside me.

"That hoss! That beast!" he groaned. "You ain't scalpin' me?" he pleaded.

It didn't take much deducing to figure this man had tried to steal Mukue. My first reaction was anger, but my pa's teachings kicked in right quickly. The man was hurting real bad. He'd paid a price for his attempted crime. "You're the lowlife that tried to steal my horse."

Now, the man was doubly fearful. He not only feared being scalped but was in the hands of the owner of the horse he'd tried to steal. Worse, he was utterly defenseless. He knew full well that horse thieves got hanged.

I smelled something offensive. The man was so fearful, he'd soiled himself. "Can you stand?" I was managing to contain my anger fairly well, but also wished I had a bandana to cover my nose from his stench.

"M...my...leg be busted," he responded.

I looked at his legs, but they didn't appear out of sorts. Maybe he'd been kicked in his knee real bad. I noticed the riding quirt lying in the dust beside his leg. "You're going to stand, or I'll scalp you where you lie."

His eyes widened even more. He reached out his hand for help, then pulled it back in fear of me. He finally got a leg under himself, and using the wall as support, inched his way to a standing position. He still struggled to breathe, having likely had a couple of ribs broken by Mukue. "Whatcha gonna do?" he pleaded.

I knew exactly what I was going to do. Bandera had a sheriff. This man might not hang, but there'd be a penalty for attempted horse stealing. "Ease up. I'm not scalping you, though you earned it."

"You be an Injun'?" he asked.

Now, I smiled. "It's your lucky day. You're dealing with the White part of me." How on earth I found humor in the situation was beyond me. I wanted to get him to the Bandera jail, but it was well past midnight. What would I do with this ne'er-do-well until daylight?

"Y...yuh be a breed?!" He reflexively doubled over in pain as he uttered the words.

I so wanted to slug this despicable excuse for a human, but I held back. I took a calming breath. "What's your name?"

The would-be thief looked at me through his red-rimmed eyes. "Dakota Durant," he responded. "Folk call me Kota," he added. "Where we goin'?"

"We're heading back to the stable. The jail is across the street, and that's where you'll be come morning." I grabbed his elbow and nudged him toward the street.

With his supposedly broken leg, it was slow going. I wanted to shove him, but didn't want to be picking him up from the dusty street.

Kota limped along gamely. We came to a water trough in front of the stable, so I doused him from the waist down to get rid of his decidedly foul odor. It helped, though he was none too pleased.

Considering his condition, I was hopeful we'd reach the stable before sunrise. As it was, it took nearly a half hour to walk that couple of hundred yards. Once at the stable, I fetched a rope from a hook and bound Kota's hands behind him. I eased him into the hay. By now, he'd passed out, so I dragged him near Pa and Peter, then rejoined Mukue in the stall. I think he sensed that he'd been avenged.

* * *

I was awakened at sunrise by Peter. "What's that varmint you must have dragged in here last night?"

I was a tad groggy. "Horse thief," I said squinty-eyed. I shook off the cobwebs. "Make that an attempted horse thief. Reckon to turn him over to the sheriff this morning."

Pa joined us. "You sure he's the one?" he asked.

"The cut up the side of his head was made by a horseshoe. He's got busted ribs from being kicked, his knee is nearly broken, and a riding quirt was beside his leg when I found him. He's carrying the evidence on his body. Also, I reckon the stable boy will recognize him."

"Well, the sheriff here is Buck Hamilton. I hear tell that he's a fair sort as sheriffs go," noted Pa. "Let's haul the rascal to the jail and then grab breakfast. We'll chat with that rancher fellow Klappenbach mentioned and then head home."

We went back to the front of the stable, where Kota lay with his hands still tied behind his back.

About this time, the stable boy strolled in. He looked to have been tended to by someone, as his wounds were bandaged. One eye was swollen shut, but he was in good spirits. "Yuh got him!" he exclaimed.

"He the one?" I pressed.

The stable boy nodded vigorously.

"Snitch," muttered Kota, as he awakened.

I smiled. "You're going to regret ever touching my horse, Dakota Durant."

Peter and I lifted him and mostly dragged him across the street to the jail. Pa led the way, and the stable boy followed. There was a light on inside, so we invited ourselves inside with Kota in tow.

Sheriff Hamilton was at his desk, shuffling papers and working on a cup of rotgut coffee. He looked up to find his office full of mostly strangers. "Uh, to what do I owe this honor?" he queried.

My pa stepped forward. "We have a guest for one of your cells, Sheriff. This Dakota Durant here attempted to steal a horse. We caught him with evidence and a witness."

Hamilton looked up. "I know this man. He's no horse thief."

"Excuse me?" I responded.

Hamilton smiled. "Just joking. Whose horse did Mr. Durant try to steal?"

"My son's horse, Sheriff," replied my pa.

"The big bay?" he asked.

We all nodded.

Hamilton looked at Kota. "Anyone with half a brain that knows horses could've told you that horse was a one-man bronc. And it sure looks like you paid a steep price."

"I saw it happen," volunteered the stable boy.

Hamilton shook his head. "Wasn't that long ago, you'd be hanging from one of those trees out yonder, Durant. As it is, they'll reserve a place for you over in Huntsville."

I knew that Huntsville was host to a Texas state prison. "We must head back north, Sheriff," I said. "I suppose he's all yours."

"Just one more thing. I'll need a signed statement from you. While you're writing that, I'll park Mr. Durant in a cell."

I wrote a statement and signed it. I referenced the stable boy as witness, and he signed with an *X*.

With the attempted horse theft wrapped up, we headed to breakfast. Naturally, that was at Klappenbach's place.

After chatting with the rancher Klappenbach had referred us to, we saddled up and headed ourselves back to Rising Cross Ranch. By now, I'd discussed my plans with Pa, and he was agreeable. Peter would head up the construction of the first ranch buildings and corrals. We'd be neighbors, so he had a vested interest in the endeavor.

* * *

Pa wasn't able to hold back his curiosity any longer. "Son, where are you getting the money to do all this?"

Peter's head swung around. Surely, he'd been wondering the same thing but didn't reckon to challenge his older brother.

I'd had the good sense to not carry the pouch of gold nuggets with me from Wyoming. I'd been taught to always be truthful and that even a half-truth contained a partial lie. There was really no way to hide this truth, especially from my pa. "I profited from the sale of Quarter Horses," I replied lamely.

Pa gave me the look that said he was expecting more. He knew full-well that we hadn't sold enough horses to pay for a ranch and livestock.

I swallowed hard. "There's gold on the Laramie Cross Breed Ranch." There, I'd said it.

Peter's and Pa's jaws dropped. "Is there a lot?" pressed Pa.

"Enough," I responded. "Nobody up there knows except Awentia and our boys. Moses and Michael aren't talking," I added with a grin.

"God sure has been good to you, Isa," extolled Peter. "Pray it continues."

That left us to travel silently onward, each taken with

our thoughts on my good fortune. We all knew that Pa and Ma had brought us up to share in God's bounty. While our family would benefit from the treasure, we would ensure that it had a positive impact on those around us. It occurred to me that it was a stark contrast to the greed-driven gold seekers and equally-greedy opportunists in places like Deadwood, South Dakota, or Sutter's Mill, California.

Finally, Pa spoke up, "Good to keep it a secret, son. Never pull too much at any one time, as folks get suspicious right easily."

"I'm letting it lie for now, Pa," I replied.

"You might be thinking on filing what they call a placer claim to protect your rights. I don't know what the laws are in Wyoming." Pa scratched his chin thoughtfully. "Of course, once you file a claim with the government, you can be sure that the whole world will know of your find. You're likely right to keep it a secret for now."

It was reassuring that my pa shared my own thinking as to the gold. It had also occurred to me that, if I found gold nuggets so easily, there was a fair-to-middling chance there were similar deposits in the area around my ranch. The last thing we needed was a gold rush. The steady stream of wagons headed west on the Oregon Trail was plenty. We sure didn't need another boom town springing up in our backyard.

# Chapter 20

## Trouble Again

I must admit that it wasn't easy leaving Rising Cross Ranch, having missed my folks more than I'd realized. Ma packed some delicious vittles for the trail. Of course, they were too good to last all that long. What folks called delay gratification was a nonstarter so far as my ma's cooking.

The goodbyes weren't long enough, as I headed Mukue up the trail, followed by Bertrum on a tether and Taabe. The trip had been profitable if only to see my family, though I looked forward to being back in Morning Star's arms.

Reaching the Pinta Trail, I reckoned to have a couple of hours before sunset. It would give me plenty of time to find a place to spend the night.

Sure enough, it wasn't long before I came upon a place that had clearly been used many times by travelers. The site had plenty of forage for Mukue and Bertrum and featured a cleared-out area with a small lean-to of pine branches. If it rained, I'd be afforded some protection.

As I sat chowing down on the vittles my ma had prepared, I got to thinking about these wide-open spaces folks referred to as the frontier. As I understood the legends, my grandfather's people had settled this land many centuries ago, long before the White man arrived. The land was wide and the people few, so the *numunuu* claimed no ground as theirs. Tribal holdings were measured in terms of hunting grounds, the areas in which tribes could support their hunts for food. Where there was competition for good hunting grounds, tribes would fight each other. Warriors would do battle, while counting coup, killing, and taking captives as slaves. Yet, boundaries were so vast as to be indefensible. Tribes fought over hunting grounds and later for access to the best trading opportunities. If bored, warriors might simply fight to take scalps and have stories to tell their children at campfires. As White settlers came, the tribes began to realize that they faced a threat that would not be defeated in battle. Were they settlers or intruders? No matter. They kept coming. The Whites killed many buffalo, brought disease, and defended themselves with powerful weapons, but they also brought opportunity. The cultures clashed for many decades until the tribes begrudgingly accepted the White man's ways, while holding on to some vestiges of their own heritage. I realized that I was in-between the White world and the Red world. I was from the union of my White pa and Comanche ma, so had the blood of both cultures in me. As I reflected, I figured that it mostly worked to my advantage.

There were prejudiced folks around to be sure. I'd encountered some yet managed to survive. I suspect that God must have some use for me that he'd kept me around thus far. Nevertheless, this was still America's western frontier. It was a mostly lawless place, though that was in the process of changing as ever more folks settled the wilds and built towns, ranches, and farms.

* * *

The breaking sun and heavy dew told me it would be a blistering hot day. Blessedly, this part of my journey offered plenty of water. It'd be tougher going when I reached the Texas Panhandle. A time or two, I ran into a newfangled invention that was beginning to find its way onto Texas ranchlands. Pa had warned me that it was coming. They called it barbed wire. I saw it as carving up freedom with every twist of its rusting wires. Where boundaries had once been established simply by handshakes between men, they'd now be set by this thorny wire. More than tearing a man's clothing or cutting a careless steer, it stuck in the very craw of Texas soil.

I made my way up the Pinta Trail, wending my way past oak, elm, mesquite, and occasional magnolia. It seemed a shame that I'd missed the magnolia's pretty white flowers. It was a ready reminder that the first week of September had arrived. While the heat would make for slow going, I reckoned we'd still manage to reach home by early October. I chuckled to myself that we'd arrive well before winter's blasts.

I hadn't encountered any travelers thus far, but remained cautious. You never could be sure as to what lurked around the next bend in the trail.

Mukue was enjoying a brief respite from me sitting on his back, as we reached a high point that offered a beautiful view of the surrounding hills. I paused to take in the natural beauty. I'd come to realize that such pauses to drink in the land brings a peace to my soul. It filled me with what no man should ever lose: dignity. It was as though I was communing with God. In pretty much every sense, I was free. No one or no thing owned me save my Creator, and even He gave me free will.

My séance with the beauty of my surroundings was interrupted, as I caught sight of a rather large black bear. I recalled that the black bears had shorter claws than the grizzlies, but could do plenty of damage. The shorter claws were adapted to climbing trees to get at foliage. Mukue's nostrils flared as he picked up the scent. I stroked his forehead to settle him. The bear was digging into the bark, likely leaving his sign as a challenge to other bears in his territory. I saw him sniff the air. Being downwind, he'd likely picked up our scent. He was a big boar but didn't appear to be looking for trouble from humans this day. Shucks, it was really too hot to be looking to start a fuss.

As the day wore on, I felt as though I'd taken a dip in that swimming hole back at the Rising Cross Ranch. I'd shed my buckskins and donned a breechcloth and lightweight vest. The Comanche in me leaned toward practicality toward beating the heat. I thought on how folks joked that it was so hot that you could fry an egg on a rock. They weren't far from the truth this day.

I followed the mostly-dry Pedernales River, but skirted Fredericksburg. Seeing me coming clothed as I was, I chuckled to myself that they might have suspected a Comanche attack.

Once clear of Fredericksburg and that gigantic pink boulder to its north called Enchanted Rock, my path began to flatten out. I was still disinclined to meet Charles Goodnight, so bypassed the JA Ranch to the east. After leaving the remains of Adobe Walls behind me, I entered lands that were the very definition of flat, hot, and dry. Nevertheless, Mukue and Bertrum were holding up quite well. Mukue seemed none the worse for his encounter back in Bandera, though he was very definitely a one-man horse. I pitied any poor soul that tried what that Durant fellow had attempted.

* * *

Slowly but surely, we made our way northward, soon crossing what there was of this part of the Arkansas River. The dried grasses of the pancake-flat prairie stretched away before me until they met the distant azure sky. The land was wide open. No boundaries.

I reckoned I was pushing better than thirty miles a day riding from sunup to sundown. I never felt so free. Yet, I yearned to be home with my beloved Morning Star. Our souls were as one, enjoying a freedom in our togetherness.

The landscape soon transitioned to gently rolling hills, from which a traveler could see for many miles at their crests. We used to avoid riding the ridges of such hills, as it wouldn't do to offer hostiles a silhouetted target. Today? Well, I didn't reckon to encounter roving bands of Indians. As I understood it, even the Arapaho had settled down.

I suppose that I was still an inviting target for some seedy character looking for a great horse and some trifles from the pack tied to Bertrum's. Ma had packed some goodies for Morning Star and the boys. I'd shared with her about Chester Donovan and Pearl, so she'd included a gift for them.

We passed within spitting distance of the spot where Cheyenne and Arapaho had been massacred in what they called the Sand Creek Massacre back in 1864. I was still a little shave back then so had little or no appreciation for such horror. The significance meant more now, as the *numunuu* went to reservations. My little caravan had crossed the aptly-named Big Sandy a while back and now had Fort Morgan in our sights. The terrain had grown rougher, as we came upon the foothills of the Rocky Mountains. Far off to my west would be Front Range and Longs Peak.

The weather had become far cooler. I rather appreciated having traveled clear of the oppressive heat. There were more trees as well. Shade is good...mostly. Trees meant that I had to be more vigilant. On the open prairie, a man could see great distances. The consequence of that was that a traveler generally got plenty of forewarning of impending trouble. Mountains, hills, or flatlands, the land could be downright unforgiving to the unwary.

It struck me that we're pretty much naked out here on America's frontier. There are laws, but most didn't reach this far out, so far as enforcement owing to the very vastness of the landscape and few towns with any semblance of governance. It yet remained a place for the strong of heart and soul with the will to carve a life from its virgin hide. The men that the land didn't devour might be good or evil, but their common denominator was the will to survive.

Days rolled over into days, and I trekked on. I killed deer and small mammals for food and even took the time to mix some pemmican. My fires were necessarily kept small and in places where they'd be unlikely to be seen.

The terrain grew ever rougher. There were more

trees, and the hills were bigger. Maybe it was because I was off any beaten trail, but I saw nary a soul. There was plenty of game. Buffalo still roamed, and I saw elk herds and a few pronghorns. A couple of times, grizzlies sighted me but stayed clear. There were probably mountain lions out there, and while there were surely wolves, the only one I saw was Taabe.

I was half-tempted to read *The Deerslayer* again, but felt as though I'd gotten all I could from the story short of memorizing it. I did promise myself to borrow another James Fenimore Cooper book from Guernsey at the earliest opportunity.

The hills were beautiful. Gazing off at the distant mountains cast gray by the mists, I thought on the stories they held of Lakota and Cheyenne reaping its bounty and those that followed, no less harvesters of its gifts.

I crossed the South Platte River near to where Fort Morgan used to be. What remained of the fort had been auctioned off, and what wasn't used by folks to build homes and businesses was pretty-much reclaimed by the wilderness. The river was running low, so crossing was right-easy. Now, I found myself headed to more serious terrain.

I crested a hill and noted a far-off stand of aspen. I found aspen to be right pretty as trees went. In a stiff breeze, their leaves fluttered like glittering jewels. I'd seen elk and especially beaver chew deep into the bark. I was sort of daydreaming, as I appreciated the beauty of those aspens reaching high toward the sun. They were sort of a metaphor for my own striving, as though pursuing a greater goal. I was on low ground between two gentle hills between the stands of aspen. I took a quick look around and decided it was time for a break. I had a hankering for a cup of coffee, so built a small fire. Amazingly, after better than four weeks on the trail, I still had a goodly amount of the coffee my ma packed for me. I unsaddled Mukue and gave both he and Bertrum an opportunity to graze a bit on the lush grasses that abounded.

Coffee thirst slaked, I saddled Mukue and remounted. I turned uphill to get my bearings. From that vantage point, I was able to take a sweeping look around me. Off to my right, to the east, if you will, I thought I saw the glint of sunshine on metal. Was it a threat? Was it an illusion? I stared hard for a couple of minutes at the spot from where it had appeared, but there was nothing so far as I could tell. There were no indications of danger from Mukue, Bertrum, or Taabe. Nevertheless, my intuition—which rarely failed me—told me to be on guard. I slipped the Spencer from its scabbard and reckoned to ride the next few miles with it setting across my saddle horn.

I decided it might not be a good idea to ride the crests of hills, as I'd be a target if something was stalking me out there. I caught sight of some places where horses had trodden. They were shod, so unlikely to have been Indians. So far as I could tell, there were two horses. There was no sign of a packhorse or mule, which got me figuring that the two were in a hurry to wherever they headed.

I crossed a small, nearly dry creek and headed Mukue up along the side of the next hill. A stand of aspen loomed ahead, and I figured to ride through rather than around. I didn't see Taabe stop with ears erect and snout pointed ahead of us. Even Mukue hadn't indicated any danger, so I was clueless when a shot rang out, and I felt something hot slam into my shoulder. It nearly knocked me from my saddle. I was momentarily stunned. A glance at my now throbbing shoulder revealed blood. It finally occurred to me that I'd been shot. A second bullet buzzed past my ear, and I slid half stunned from Mukue with my Spencer carbine still in hand. I dove behind a fallen log. Mukue and Bertrum seemed to sense the danger and back-trailed a short distance.

Another bullet splintered bark near my head. It was too close for comfort. Sneaking a look at my shoulder, I realized that the first bullet had gone clear through the muscle and was bleeding pretty good. I stuffed my bandana inside my shirt to plug the bullet holes as much as I could. I was hunkered down behind that log and dearly wanted to see where the shooting came from. Whoever was out there had a bead on me. This was not good. Two more bullets hit the log. They were fired too close together to have come from a single gun. That meant that there were two bushwhackers out there. If one of them decided to come around behind me, I was done for. I could only pray that they weren't that smart.

I took in my surroundings as best I could. There was another log nestled between two boulders a couple of body lengths behind me. It afforded better cover, but getting there would be risky. My shoulder hurt terribly now, but I managed to crawl to the end of the log and peek around and take a good look at the aspen grove from where I thought the shots had been fired. All was quiet. Where were they? I poked my hat above the log. Nothing.

I got up just enough to run to the log and boulders

behind me. There were no shots fired. Had they left? What sort of a game was being played? I stood.

I eased cautiously over to Mukue, and despite the pain from my shoulder, climbed into the saddle. I headed us straight on into the stand of aspen I thought the shots had been fired from. I found the place where the two bushwhackers had set for me. There were a couple of bullet casings and what looked to be hoofprints of the same two horses I'd seen a while back. Now, I knew why they had no packhorse. Whoever they were, they traveled light.

A creek lay ahead. I took the opportunity to cleanse my wound and apply a poultice. I couldn't do much about my shirt, now sticky with my own blood. Also, I had no way to tie a bandage around my shoulder with one hand, so I would rely on my shirt to keep pressure and the poultice tightly on the wound. Wondering where the two men had gone gnawed at me. Why had they pulled back? Were they waiting for me somewhere ahead? Was I a random target, or was this planned? This was big country to find any particular person in, so I figured the attack to have been random. They likely wanted my horse and whatever I had packed on Bertrum. They'd be disappointed on both counts but likely didn't know that.

Off to the west was a forested area, sitting beneath some low-lying mountains. It was rough terrain and would be slower going, but difficult for anyone to set an ambush with a clear line of sight. It would suit this little caravan just fine.

* * *

I reckon I'd ridden about five miles through the forest cover, when a shot rang out and a bullet blasted the branch of a tree above my head. Mukue reared a bit, but I stayed in the saddle. Either the shooter's aim was terrible or it was a warning.

"Gonna git thet hoss yer ridin,' O'Toole!" came a holler from my right.

The voice sounded vaguely familiar. I stayed quiet. Not a minute after the threat, I heard a growl and a scream. Taabe had attacked someone.

"It be a wolf!" came a voice.

There was another scream. "Help me, Farley! Help!"

Farley? Farley DeGrange? Amazingly, it was the two drifters from back in Palo Duro Canyon from weeks ago. They must have given up on Deadwood and decided to head south along the Western Trail. Coming upon me was likely pure chance. Attacking me was a last gasp for survival by two desperate men.

"Can't help yuh, Kyle." Those were likely the last words Kyle Jones would ever hear, as I heard muffled pleadings dwindle away. Taabe was completing his labors.

The next thing I knew, a DeGrange was barreling toward me at full gallop. As he raised his rifle and aimed at me, his horse hit a low-lying log and tumbled forward. DeGrange and his rifle went flying.

Mukue reflexively pulled back, and Bertrum began to bawl his head off at the goings on.

DeGrange had landed not ten feet from us. He lay still. Too still. I saw that he wasn't breathing.

Taabe, mouth bloody from his encounter with Jones, appeared. He took a long sniff at DeGrange's body then sat to wait for me to come over. I dismounted and obliged my wolf friend. Upon closer inspection, it was clear that DeGrange was dead as a doornail. His head was askew at a decidedly unnatural angle. The fall had broken his neck; nearly torn it off. Other than the surprise at being tossed, he'd likely felt little or no pain.

I breathed a much-needed sigh of relief. I felt sad for these two. They'd missed opportunities for second and even third chances at life. They died as they'd lived; hopelessly lost. I fetched the shovel from Bertrum's pack and tried to carve out a grave for the two. The soil was far too rocky to dig very deep. I wound up digging a few inches, laying the bodies together, and covering them with rocks and what soil I could scrape up. At least, the coyotes or other scavengers wouldn't have an easy time of it. I found what personal items I could on the bodies and stuffed them in the saddlebags on their horses. Horses? I reckoned to simply extend my little caravan and drop everything off near Fort Laramie. I'd figured to be there in less than a week. It was on my planned route home.

My shoulder still hurt, but I was okay otherwise. I hoped and prayed that it wouldn't get infected. As I readied to mount Mukue, I heard the sound no man wants to hear in the forest. Mukue's earshot up, and Taabe growled. Too late! I turned and found myself looking up at a huge grizzly, standing nine feet tall and not ten feet away. Angry eyes and slobbering fangs gave full voice as to his intentions. He'd appeared as though from nowhere, not alerting Mukue or Taabe until he was nearly upon us. I drew my Colt and fired at point-blank range while yanking my Bowie knife from its sheath. I know my bullet hit the grizzly, but the beast charged full bore. I was face-to-chest with a huge furry ball of pure, hot-breathed fury. Three-inch claws slashed the air, as I swiped upward with my Bowie knife.

# Epilogue

The American western frontier was mostly unforgiving, a meeting of savagery and civilization. More and more towns were springing up, and they served as bellwethers to the civilizing of the frontier. *Wild Horses on the Laramie: A Life of No Boundaries* offers a peek into the courage, faith, endurance, and pure grit entailed in the conquest of the west. I decided at age fifteen that it was time to venture out on my own. Little did I know that the Great Plains Indian Wars loomed ahead. I'm eighteen now with a warrior woman wife, a child, and raising Quarter Horses in Wyoming. The world around me was a mix of the natural beauty of a rugged landscape and lurking dangers. This environment seemed to attract the best and worst of humans.

The frontier? Exactly what is the frontier? I reckon it to be the untamed boundary between the known and unknown, the majestic and sublime. It is a space of vast landscapes fostering inspiration, opportunity, and purpose. It is a metaphor of life, challenging the traveler to navigate its soul and embrace its very unfamiliarity.

Life expectancy on the frontier was nothing like today. A male Indian did well to live beyond age thirty, and women could expect to live a tad less. Little wonder that older tribesmen were highly respected. Life expectancy for Whites wasn't much better. A White man on the frontier tended not to live beyond his late thirties. Notably, the brevity of life generally meant that folks had to mature sooner. By the time a man or woman reached age fifteen or sixteen, he or she was pretty much an adult in terms of others expecting him or her to carry an adult set of responsibilities.

Indians? I am half Comanche. While I've dealt with Kiowa, Arapaho, Crow, Cheyenne, Shoshone, and Ute, most of my experience has been with the Comanche and Lakota peoples. Dangers? Anthropology-minded folks claim there were as many as thirteen distinct tribes of Comanche from the Quahadi or "antelope eaters" in the north to the Penateka or "honey eaters" in the south. Mix in Kiowa, Apache, and Tonkawa, and settlers had their hands full. The very name Comanche loosely translates in the Ute tribal language as *kumantsi* or "enemy." Capture by the Comanche invariably led to terrible outcomes. A fearsome lot these tribes were. The horse coupled with a long history of trade for the latest weapons and farm-grown foods in and around the Comancheria produced a highly aggressive nomadic culture heavily dependent on the buffalo. For example, Penateka Comanche Chief Buffalo Hump led more than 600 warriors on a raid through the heart of Texas in August 1840, murdering Texans, looting the city of Victoria, and looting and burning Linnville on their march to the Gulf of Mexico. It was not until 1858 that Texas Ranger John Salmon "Rip" Ford led the force of 102 heavily-armed Texas Rangers and 100 Indian allies that brought the Comanche to their knees at the Battle of Little Robe Creek on the Canadian River in Oklahoma, as described in my pa's Frontier Chronicle *Warpath: Jack's Faith is Tested.*

The northwestern plains were peopled by many tribes but especially the Sioux, comprised of three groups: Dakota, Nakota, and Lakota. The Lakota were made up of seven subgroups: Oglalas (famed for Red Cloud and Crazy Horse), Hunkpapas (famed for Sitting Bull), Miniconjous (People Who Live Near Water), Oohenunpas (Two Kettles), Itazipacolas (No Bows), Brulés (Burnt Thighs), and Sihásapas (Blackfeet). The Lakota history was no less combative than Comanche or Cheyenne. Despite the violence of the frontier, it's notable that the Lakota held to a worthy set of virtues, especially generosity, courage, fortitude, and wisdom. The North Platte country referred to in *Wild Horses on the Laramie: A Life of No Boundaries* was part of the Wyoming Territory established in 1868.

The wolf plays an important role in Wolf's Tales, both in terms of my Comanche name, Isa, translating to wolf and to my furry canine companion Taabe. There are many misconceptions of wolves. The Indians venerated them for their loyalty, power, courage, ferocity, sagacity, and devoted to family. I am sensitive to ranchers viewing wolves as a scourge that kills their cattle and to hunters who seek the elk, buffalo, deer, and moose upon which wolves prefer to prey. I certainly don't want wolves killing my livestock. The wolf is nevertheless part of the struggle between predator and prey. It could be said that life and death in the wild are part of its wonder. God gave each animal its allotted lifespan. How far does mankind go in tipping the balance one way or another?

There were plenty of wild animals on the frontier. I

do refer to bison as buffalo. Just for the record, bison and buffalo are quite different. Visualize the water buffalo and then the shaggy, awkward bulk of the American bison. Seems that "buffalo" came into common usage in America to refer to the bison, so I've chosen to use buffalo in my writings. Notable, too, is that the evasive four-legged critter many unwary folks refer to as an antelope is properly called a pronghorn. Catch one if you can. There is also a big predatory cat that most folks in North America call a mountain lion, but also answers to puma, cougar, or panther.

Historically notable in the Wolf's Tales is that the longest and most used cattle trail was the Great Western Trail from 1874 to 1893. It ran from Matamoros, Mexico, to Val Marie, Canada. As many as three hundred thousand cattle each year would eventually be driven up that Great Western Trail, especially by the likes of famed rancher Charles Goodnight.

I enjoyed no modern creature comforts. The invention of telephones was decades into the future. Transportation? Horses, mules, and oxen—ridden or pulling wagons—were the vehicles of choice. I enjoyed no refrigerator to preserve sweet treats. There were no flush toilets or showers. Folks mostly ate what grazed upon or grew from the land. Learning was squeezed from the few books that might be found, especially the Holy Bible. Can't say as the living of the era was luxurious unless you counted the sheer grandeur of majestic landscapes and of nights so quiet you could hear the stars twinkling. To fully appreciate the place, you simply had to love the incredible beauty of the outdoors. Fishing the meandering Guadalupe River in Texas or the chill waters of Wyoming's North Platte and Laramie Rivers, taking in the grandeur of Yellowstone National

Park, hunting deer and pronghorn, raising cattle and horses, and reaping the bounteous yield of the rich soil was sheer joy for a courageous visionary few. For a teen on the frontier, life could be pretty good…mostly. Otherwise, it was downright dangerous.

Thus far, I was quickly growing to manhood. My vision quest had led me on a path known only to God. I was striving to conquer personal fears and prejudices, fight Indians and bandits, defend against wild beasts, travel the wild country, and drive cattle and horses. With it, I found the love of my life and a life purpose. As you have seen, I especially draw upon my faith and what I was taught by my parents. And yet, all of this is constantly tested. I had to learn to trust in instincts forged from my biblical and life lessons. Yes, I'm on a frontier adventure and more. And you, dear reader, will now be able to follow me, Isa O'Toole, as I seek my own way in life and share my adventures. May God ever bless Morning Star and me.

# Glossary

## Definitions

**Bear sign**—Cowboy slang for donuts.

**Big Father or Great Father**—All-powerful Indian deity.

**Bota bag**—A canteen fashioned from leather and popular among Indians, mountain men, and many travelers of the western frontier.

**Cold Camp**—Camp without a campfire, generally done to avoid the smoke that might alert threats.

**Dog run**—The sheltered space or breezeway between two sections of some southern ranch houses. Living quarters were usually on one side and sleeping quarters on the other.

**Fletch**—The fin-shaped bird feathers on an arrow that help stabilize its flight.

**Gallery**—A synonym for porch. Folks in the west often called the structures across the front of their homes galleries.

**Life debt**—A cultural phenomenon in which

someone whose life is saved or spared by another becomes indebted or in some way connected to their savior.

**Pemmican**—Lean dried strips of meat pounded into a paste, mixed with fat and berries, and then pressed into small cakes.

**Possibles bag (aka parfleche)**—A leather or canvas sack carried by cowboys and containing essentials like soap, matches, bandages, extra spurs, smoke makings, and playing cards

**Remuda**—A herd of horses frequently deployed on trail drives and by Plains Indians.

**Rendezvous**—Annual celebratory gathering of mountain men.

**Sand**—Courage.

**Shaman**—Medicine man.

**Teepee**—An enclosed conical transportable shelter constructed of long poles and buffalo hides with a vent at the top to permit smoke to escape.

**Travois**—A wedge-shaped structure constructed of two poles and a cross-beam lashed together and dragged behind horses, mules, or dogs by Plains Indians.

**Wahg!**—Mountain man version of hail the camp or hello.

## COMANCHE TRANSLATIONS

**Aitu**—Not good

**Ana o'a hi'it**—Phrase for "desire to eat"

**Ap**—Father

**Aruka**—Deer

**Eetu**—Bow

**Ekakwitsubaitu**—Lightning

**Ekapitu**—Red

**Eekasahpana paraiboo**—Army officer (soldier chief)

**Haa**—Yes

**Hawokatu**—Hollow, loose

**Hoikwa**—Hunt, look for prey

**Isa**—Wolf

**Isa wasu**—Poison

**Kaahaniitu**—deceive, cheat

**Kahni**—Life

**Kamakuna**—Loved one

**Kee**—No

**Kobe**—Wild horse

**Kohto**—Build a fire

**Kooitu**—Die

**Kuha**—Hello

**Kuhmabai**—Married

**Kuisa**—Coyote

**Kuuna**—Fire

**Kuya akatu**—Afraid of

**Kwakuru**—Defeat someone

**Kwihnai**—Eagle

**Mua**—Moon

**Mukue**—Spirit

**Nahuu**—Knife

**Natsuitu**—Strong

**NiyáŋkA**—We eat

**Numu**—Cow, Cattle

**Numunahkahnis**—Family

**Numunuu**—Referring to the members of the Comanche tribes. Literally: people.

**Ohapitu**—Yellow

**Onaa**—Son or daughter

**Paa**—Water

**Pabi**—Friend

**Paaka**—Arrow

**Peeka**—Kill

**Pia**—Mother

**Pia huutsuu**—Bald eagle

**Pia wa'óo**—Comanche words for mountain lion, puma, or cougar.

**Pihi**—Heart

**Pohya** (or poya)—Walk

**Puuka**—Horse

**Sunipu**—Medicine (as in strong medicine)

**Suumaru**—Ten

**Taa Narumi**—Master; God

**Taabe**—Sun

**Tabu**—Coward

**Tamu**—Rabbit

**Tasiwoo**—Buffalo

**Tenahpu**—Man

**Tomoobi**—Sky

**Tosa**—White man or woman

**Tosaabitu**—White

**Totsiyaa**—Flower

**Tumah tuyai**—After life

**Tuhibitu**—Black

**Tumhyokenu**—Believe, trust

**Tu Taiboo**—Black man

**Umaru**—Rain

**Unha haksi nahniaka**—Phrase for "what's your name?"

**Wa'ipu**—Woman

**Wasápe**—Bear

**Wutsutsuki**—Rattlesnake

## LAKOTA TRANSLATIONS

**Ate**—Father

**Ayústan**—Abandon, retreat, leave

**Enákiya**—Stop

**Hau, mitákuye oyás'e**—Welcome

**Igmuwatogla**—Mountain lion

**Ínyan**—Fire

**Isan**—Knife

**Iya Tate**—Wind

**Iyaya**—Go, leave

**Jiji**—Light hair

**Katá**—Kill

**Kola**—Friend (male)

**Kize**—Fight

**Maka**—The earth and grandmother of all things

**Mas'óphiye**—Trade or barter

**Mato**—Bear, also eat

**Mini**—Water

**Nagi**—The spirit that has never been a man

**Nanji**—Jealous

**Niya**—Ghost

**Okin**—Pretty

**Oyate**—The people or nation

**Sapa**—Black

**Ska**—White

**Scan**—Sky

**Sunkawaka**—Horse

**Sunkmanitu tanka**—Wolf

**Takuwe**—Why

**Tanka**—Wolf

**Tatanka**—The great beast (patron of health, ceremonies, provision)

**Unk**—Created by Maka; embodies all evil beings

**Unktehi**—One who kills
**Wakan Tanka**—God (monotheistic)
**Wamaka nagi**—Animal spirit
**Wanbli**—Eagle
**Wani**—Four winds (weather)
**Wasake**—Strong
**Wash tay**—Good
**Wasichus**—White man
**Wasna**—Pemmican
**Wi**—The sun (chief of all gods)
**Wica**—Complete man
**Wicasa**—Man (gender)
**Wicasa wakan**—Shaman
**Wiiya**—Danger
**WiiyakA**—Marry
**Wiiyuka**—Coward
**Wiiyukta**—Love
**Winyan**—Woman
**Wowahwa**—Peace
**Zuzeca**—Snake

# Watch For: Wyoming Destiny: Hope Triumphs Over Fate

(The Wolf's Tales 4)

**AVAILABLE IN SPRING 2026**

Want to make sure you don't miss the release? Sign up for our Wise Wolf Books newsletter at www.wisewolfbooks.com

# Thank You

Thank you for taking the time to read *Wild Horses on the Laramie: A Life of No Boundaries.* If you enjoyed it, please consider telling your friends or posting a short review. Word of mouth is an author's best friend and much appreciated.

Thank you.
*Mark Greathouse*

# Acknowledgments

Authoring books doesn't simply happen in a vacuum. The author provides the creative talent and crafts the stories, but there's so much more that demands acknowledgment. There are lots of folks and places that contribute to my authoring endeavors. So it is with *Wild Horses on the Laramie: A Life of No Boundaries.* The tale is set in 1879 and transitions into 1880, sharing the trials and tribulations of a young man forced to meet the challenges inherent in the dangerous vastness of the western frontier. But this novel stands apart. At its core, it is also about the taming of that frontier. The protagonist epitomizes the freedom of America's western frontier and represents a final bastion of honor in America. This tale follows Jack O'Toole's earlier Frontier Chronicles series, beginning with his adventures in *Perilous Trails: Jack's Adventure Begins.* Hopefully, readers will find this second book in the Wolf's Tales series worthy of their time and emotional involvement. Saddle up and ride into the future with Isa O'Toole.

I've been blessed with many friends and family who have supported my writings. My wife Carolyn's reviews and encouragement were a huge help, along with very important tech support from our sons Mike and Matt. Thanks to my pastor, Randy, for their faith insights. Many more friends and family have contributed support at some level to the creation and publication of my Wolf's Tales, be it encouragement or advice.

Naturally, I am major grateful to the great folks at the Wise Wolf Books imprint of Wolfpack Publishing. The team they bring to publishing is first-rate in editing, cover design, and the myriad tasks that lead to successful book sales.

It's only right to acknowledge my ancestors. They were actual settlers of the South Texas frontier. In addition to inspiring me, they provided a quite helpful true-to-life framework as to the life and times on the Texas Nueces Strip. I've also personally walked the very landscapes traversed by my fictional and historical characters.

Most of my authoring has occurred in my office as decorated to channel my inner Texan, but my creative juices have often been inspired and imagination stoked in cafés and coffee houses across America. My favorites were Hester's Café & Coffee Bar in Corpus Christi, TX; Nueces Café in Robstown, TX; Java Ranch Espresso Bar & Café in Fredericksburg, TX; PAX Coffee & Goods in Kerrville, TX; Ragged Edge Coffee House and Bantam Coffee Roasters in Gettysburg, PA; 1889 Coffee House in Helena, MT; Wild Joe's Coffee Shop, Bozeman, MT; Tumbleweed Café, Gardiner, MT; Dunn Brothers Coffee in Rapid City, SD; Postmasters Coffee & Bakery and Brio Coffeehouse in Waynesboro, PA; Birdie's Café and American Ice Co Café in Westminster, MD; Deja Brew Coffee House, New Oxford and Deja Brew at Miney Branch, Carroll Valley, PA; Baltimore Coffee & Tea Co., Frederick Coffee Company & Café, and Dublin Roasters in Frederick, MD; Qualle Café and Grounded Coffee & Bakery, Cherokee, NC; Palace Café, Amarillo, TX; and Unto Others Café, Lamar, CO. I must admit to also frequenting a few Dunkin Donuts and Starbucks around our fine nation. The décors and easy listening music in these fine establishments, combined with savory cups of coffee, tended to set me in the right creative frame of mind. They also afforded engagement with many fine citizens of our nation.

Last but not least, I'm especially thankful for the many folks who have read and enjoyed my books.

I do believe it's important to acknowledge how the old west represents the brave pioneering spirit of settlers who met the challenges and transcended mere survival to enable America to achieve exceptional growth. The settling of the American frontier west is replete with tales of leveraging freedom for individual achievement. I hope you'll agree that reliving our past—even through history-based fiction—often has the effect of pointing the way to an ever-brighter future. Might we be up to it? I hope that the inspiration I've drawn from my having walked the very earth my characters have trodden, coupled with my extensive historical research, will enable readers to fully experience the grit, adventure, and passion of my characters while sensing aromas of gunsmoke, trail dust, leather, and bluebonnets.

Thanks kindly to all of you, and please do enjoy *Wild Horses on the Laramie: A Life of No Boundaries.*

# About the Author

Award-winning author Mark Greathouse's love for the western genre draws upon his deep family roots and love of the outdoors honed from teen years hiking the Appalachian Trail and family travels across America's frontier. Greathouse began writing full time after a successful career as a business executive and later as an entrepreneurial investor and advisor. His service as president of several business and community nonprofits led to their extraordinary growth. He holds a BA in English and MBA in marketing. Greathouse donates time and books annually to support wounded military warriors.

A member of Western Writers of America and the Wild West History Association, he also contributes articles on the history of America's west to western-themed magazines. Greathouse was recognized as a 2024 Finalist in western genre by the American Literary Book Awards for his sixth Tumbleweed Saga, *Nueces Truth: Texans Face War's Realities.*

His *Frontier Chronicles,* a series of western novels aimed at adventure-minded teens and young adults while weaving a Christian message within their fabric, are aimed at lighting fires of truth, faith, hope, and life purpose in the bellies of today's teen boys and girls. Just as seeds must be sown to reap the harvest, so the seeds of faith must be planted to raise tomorrow's men and women.

www.ingramcontent.com/pod-product-compliance
Lightning Source LLC
LaVergne TN
LVHW091128080826
845145LV00008B/2087